C   — SWOPE PARENTE

TWIST
OF
FATE

Spectacle Publishing

An e-book edition of this book was published in 2012 by Spectacle Publishing Media Group, LLC.

Spectacle Publishing Media Group books may be purchased for educational, business, or sales promotional use. For information please write:

Special Marketing,
Spectacle Publishing Media Group
P.O. Box 295,
Lisle, NY 13797

FIRST SPECTACLE PAPERBACK PUBLISHED 2012

Author photo by Aleda Johnson Powell

Design by Rob Gee

ISBN 978-1-938444-02-9

ACKNOWLEDGEMENTS

This book and the additional books in the series would not have been written if we had not received encouragement from Allyn Swope Stotz. Allyn, by pursuing her dream of writing children's books and making that dream come true, showed us that the only obstacle to doing what you really want is not trying. We'd like to thank her for inspiring us, and for continuing to provide the encouragement that fed our momentum.

One of the lessons we learned quickly is that much research goes into putting together a novel. We were fortunate to locate people willing to share their expertise and time. Mark Swope used his Internet research capabilities to help us find information on a number of subjects that have gone into the book's plot. Jane and Rick Jacobs provided the background and ideas we needed for the pharmaceutical topics in this book. Elvis Bello, a police detective in the Richmond, Virginia area, and his wife Jessica took time during a busy period of their lives to answer a number of questions we had about the realities of how law enforcement pursues criminals. Thanks to all of you for giving us many hours, as well as your best wishes.

We also would like to thank our families and friends for giving this book its first read. We needed your input to continue moving forward. We are especially grateful to our husbands, Robert and Ray, and other family members who put up with our absence—sometimes mentally and sometimes physically—while we happily worked on this creative endeavor.

We were very fortunate to have worked with Editor Tammi Albright, who seemed to know just what our story needed to be better. Lastly, we want to acknowledge how grateful we are to our publisher, Spectacle Publishing Media Group, LLC. The workshops President Eric Staggs held for us provided useful new ways to think about creative writing and the fire we needed to keep writing and improving. Thanks, also to Jared Saathoff for his polishing and to Ditrie Sanchez and Shirley J. Knowles who will be a big part of moving forward with this and the upcoming books in our series.

Genilee would also like to point out to Smitty (sorry, that's Mr. Smith) from Edgerton, Ohio, that a very good English teacher can create a passion for the written word that lasts a lifetime. Finally, to the wait staff at our local Applebee's restaurant: thanks for listening to many conversations between us on how to kill off our characters!

For all the people in the world who are writers at heart, but haven't yet put words down on paper or who don't believe life will give them the time or opportunity to become authors.

Believe in your dreams, your stories, your creative abilities-and give those who love to read another channel for doing so.

The small boy's leg muscles ached. His head hurt, and he couldn't catch his breath. He'd been running for a long time, stumbling occasionally in his blind effort to get away from the policeman.

Finally, his feet simply no longer worked, and he fell hard to the ground.

He lay there for a moment, but could hear no one in pursuit, so he sat up slowly. His pants leg was torn, his knee ached. It was scraped raw where he'd hit the ground, and the boy brushed away small pebbles that had implanted in his flesh when he fell.

The boy got up and looked around. He was lost. He had been running for most of an hour through streets he'd never seen before—first from some rough boys, then the policeman. He recognized the stale odor of rotting food and the urine reek that most city alleys held, a smell that got him up off the ground and walking again.

He peeked around a dumpster to make sure he was not being pursued before leaving the foulness behind and walking into the street. The sound of a dog barking startled him and quickened his pace. He wasn't afraid of many things—he had discovered he could outrun most dangers in life, including foster fathers, strangers and most people in uniforms—but not the dogs. They had two extra legs that made them faster. The barking seemed far away, though, and the little boy relaxed, peaking into a window long enough to see a mom tossing a child into the air as both of them giggled. The image of a dark-haired woman from when he was very little came to his mind, accompanied by the memory of a sweet smell and a feeling of warmth. But though he often thought of her, the picture never lasted long.

The boy turned his head away from the window and walked straight ahead until he came to a park. His stomach grumbled as he began to search the trash cans. Three cans later, he had no food, and he was so tired, he couldn't go any further. Sighing deeply, he settled his weary body on the end of a bench. He was almost asleep when a hand touched his shoulder.

The boy's body tensed, prepared to run, but the hand held him in place. When the youngster looked up at who was holding him, however, he saw only an old man, wearing ripped clothes that were dirtier than his own. The man's face was covered with scraggly gray hair, and only a set of pale blue eyes peaked through.

"You're on my bench," the man said. His voice was scratchy and deep.

The boy trembled inside. The man was tall and scowled fiercely. But the boy would not show fear, and he certainly would not give in to the urge to cry. Crying had never gotten the boy anything but a whipping, and besides, only babies cried.

"Have you run away from home, young man?" The man's voice softened just a little. The old man withdrew his hand from the boy's shoulder and sat down a few feet away on the bench.

The boy looked around for the best way to escape.

"Do you need help finding your way home, boy?"

The boy turned his head back toward the old man. "Got no home."

"Well, boy-with-no-home, what's your name, then?" Although the beard covered much of the man's face, the boy saw the crinkles around the pale eyes that indicated the old man was smiling.

"None of your business, mister."

"Then I guess you ain't hungry youngster." The boy spotted the sack on the man's lap. The old man withdrew a long sandwich from the sack.

The boy's mouth watered at the sight. But he crossed his arms in defiance.

"Why you gotta know my name, mister?"

"Well," the man answered as he took a bite out of half and held the other half towards the boy, "If I am going to share this here sandwich, I'd like to know who I'm sharing it with."

CHAPTER ONE

Casey didn't know what she expected to see when the detective walked into the restaurant. When she'd called earlier to make the appointment, she pictured Kojak with a lollypop in his mouth and a frown on his face, or the disheveled Colombo with wrinkled trench coat and messy hair. Sam Osborne fit neither of those images. In fact, he was not particularly striking in appearance—he wasn't large or brawny, and he looked crisply dressed. But Casey noticed him as he moved across the room because he flowed with the ease of a person who knew exactly who and what he was.

Sam's five-foot-six inches were adorned

casually in a neat pair of gray slacks and a navy suit coat. His full head of light brown hair was neatly trimmed and combed. When he got close to the table, Casey saw black-rimmed glasses that rested gently on the bridge of his nose. They hid a pair of gentle hazel eyes.

He extended his hand to shake hers. "Thank you for meeting me here in the restaurant, Ms. Lewis. A broken elevator is a bit of an inconvenience when you're just starting a new business in town."

Casey waved her hand in dismissal.

"If you're new here in our neighborhood, Mr. Osborne, you need a slice of Mabel's pie, anyway. And she makes the best cup of coffee, never mind the Starbucks across the street," Casey said. "Besides, it's cozier in the restaurant." She maneuvered her wheelchair backwards and forwards until she was snug against the table.

"Please call me Sam. Yes, I've heard what Mabel's pie can do to the waistline. Maybe it's better the elevator is broken—I'll have to take the stairs," he joked.

His comment elicited a broad smile from the petite, blond girl, who seemed to relax her posture. Sam sat down across from her, and Casey turned to pour them both a cup of coffee from a carafe resting on the table.

"Frankly, Ms. Lewis, your telephone call surprised me. My new phone was just hooked up yesterday."

Sam took a sip of his coffee, and then set the cup down carefully.

"Do you really think someone is trying to kill you?" he asked.

Casey, who was blowing on her coffee, set the cup down without drinking. She glanced side to side in the restaurant, then sighed and sat back.

"I'm pretty certain of it."

"Perhaps" he said, "You could tell me why you believe someone is after you?"

"I know it sounds crazy, but believe me, it's very real, and I'm not the only person who believes this … Joseph?" She turned in her chair and beckoned to a tall, suit-adorned gray-haired gentleman who moved toward the table and sat down in the chair across from Sam.

"Detective Osborne—Sam, this is my friend Joseph Lindquist. He and his wife Sarah take care of me. Joseph, tell this gentleman what you believe about the attempts on my life." She turned towards the man, who appeared to be in his early sixties and whose brow was wrinkled with worry. Sam took a small notebook and pen out of his pocket, and set them down in front of him.

"Sarah and I have been with Casey since she was a small child," Joseph explained. "When her parents died a little over seven years ago, we moved into the house to care for her. We are very close to her and consider her our daughter, and I can tell you, Mr. Osborne, she isn't given to making up tall tales."

Sam picked up the notebook then and flipped up the cover.

"Please call me Sam. I have no reason to disbelieve what you're telling me, so fill me in on the facts."

Joseph cleared his throat and began.

"The first attempt occurred over six months ago—last summer—though we had no idea at the time it was anything but an accident."

Sam looked up at Joseph, then Casey for a moment, then he smiled and said, "Go on." His eyes returned to the notebook.

"When the weather is nice, Casey is in the habit of talking a stroll on the grounds. She insists on doing it herself without Sarah and I along." Joseph gave Casey a stern glare, but she simply covered his hand with her own.

"We've built a path designed to accommodate her wheelchair," Joseph continued, the sternness gone. "We've also built several walkouts—places where she can wheel out to look at a particularly nice spot. We've got one that hangs over the pond and another in a place on the path where the trees break and you can see a panorama of the surroundings.

"The panoramic view walkout hangs over the edge of a very steep hill, which falls several hundred feet to the next level. We hired a specialist to construct that walkout, someone who assured us it was sturdy enough to hold the weight of at least ten people, but on one of Casey's walks, it gave out on her."

Joseph shuddered, then, and Casey picked up the conversation.

"I was fortunate, really. The whole thing sort of collapsed below me, but somehow I managed to grab hold of the remaining lumber and the roots of a tree and hold on for dear life. Most of it eventually fell away, but I was able to hold on."

"When I found her more than an hour later, she was still clinging to one of the remaining supports," Joseph said. "She'd actually managed to wrap the scarf from her neck around that support as well as some of the roots of the bushes that grow on the side of the hill." He looked at Casey then, pride evident on his face, but when he turned back to Sam, his expression crumpled.

"If I hadn't come across her—"

Casey squeezed Joseph's hand.

"You did find, me, though, Joseph. And I really wasn't hurt, just very scared."

Sam looked up from his notebook and asked, "Did you wonder then why the structure would collapse? Did the police check out the site?"

"At that point we had no reason to think that it was anything but an accident—maybe faulty construction or rotted wood," Joseph said. "And we didn't think to report it. We took Casey to the hospital, found out she was okay, and then brought her back home. I wouldn't let her go on the path by herself for a while, and then I made her promise not to use the walkouts when she did. I had all the others checked out. There wasn't enough of the structure left to see what went wrong, though the foundation board is still in one piece, and we have not replaced the walkout. Casey insisted we put the whole thing out of our minds, and we would have, except for an incident that happened about a month ago, followed two weeks later by an even more bizarre event."

Joseph took a sip of his own coffee before continuing. Sam had been busily scratching notes.

"The second attempt was January thirteenth. Casey wanted to see a certain show at the theater downtown. She asked me to go with her. I dropped her off at the curb and went to park the car. She waited for me there, and I was almost back to her when I saw an SUV driving straight towards her. She couldn't see it because she was facing me. I waved and shouted as I ran towards her, but she had no idea what I was doing. The car was coming from behind her, fast. I just managed to get to her in time to push her out of the way; that car missed us both by inches and both of us were pretty shaken up."

"That's understandable. You're sure, though, that it was actually headed for her? And did you see who was at the wheel?"

"You couldn't really see into the car, or at least I didn't have time to get a good look. The side and back windows were tinted, so once the car was past, I couldn't see anything. But to tell you the truth, it happened so quickly, I wasn't thinking about who was driving. If I had been less shaken up, I would have noted the license plate. I just reacted. Sat on the curb for awhile catching my breath. I don't even know for certain what kind of car it was, but I believe it was a gray or silver SUV of some kind."

"Did you contact the police?" Sam asked.

"No, we didn't. Maybe that was foolish on our part, but it happened so fast, and to answer your other question: no, we weren't really positive it was intentional. The driver, though, never stopped to see if we were okay. The car just sped away down the street."

"There wasn't much the police could have done, anyway, unless you'd gotten a license number or maybe it took place where there was a security camera," Sam interjected.

"It might have helped to have reported it though, because two weeks later, something we are sure was an attempt on Casey's life occurred, and the police were somewhat skeptical about those first two incidents," Joseph said.

Sam looked up from his notes then, pen poised above the paper. "So what was this third attempt?"

Joseph knitted his fingers together, and put his joined fists on the table.

"This happened about two weeks later—January twenty-seventh, just last week. It was a lovely winter day, and we'd been trapped in the house for most of January. I took Casey to the park for fresh air. But I couldn't shake the feeling that we were being watched. I couldn't spot anyone, so I thought I was probably being paranoid. We were almost back to the car—"

He paused for a moment. The fists came apart, and he used one hand to rub his brow.

"Casey spotted something on the ground

and leaned over to investigate, as did I. A bird's nest had fallen from a tree. If she hadn't chosen that minute to lean forward—

"Someone shot at her, two shots. They hit the chair on one of those shots, but not Casey. She felt the chair move, and we heard the shots, but by the time we realized what had happened, I was in a state of panic. I grabbed the chair and just started running for cover. We were close to the garage, and that's where I headed. By the time I got there, I finally thought to look around for the shooter, but I never saw anyone."

Sam scratched his head and asked, "Where do the police say the shooter was?"

"An alley close to the garage, so in hindsight, it may not have been wise to head that way, but you don't think, you just head for the nearest building," Joseph said.

"We found out after the police arrived and talked to us that the second bullet hit the tree just to the side of where Casey sat in her chair. It's pretty much a miracle she wasn't hit. The police recovered the bullet, but neither Casey nor I saw anyone. At the time, they said the shooting might not be related to us at all, though they promised to look into it. The theater isn't in a very good neighborhood. We told them about the other incidents but we didn't really have anything specific to give them."

Joseph sat back in his chair then, his hands again on the table.

"But Sam, even if the police think we're nuts, we *know* Casey is being targeted by someone, and she needs more help and protection than we can give her—especially now," Joseph said.

Casey broke into the conversation to explain. "That's the reason I told you on the phone I need a bodyguard, Sam. Joseph and Sarah need to visit her sister, which means they will be out of town for awhile. Sarah's sister, Lucy, is about to go through a major heart operation, and she needs her sister at her side. But with these attempts on my life, Joseph and Sarah refuse to leave me."

She poured more coffee for herself then and added just a touch of cream. She raised her eyes to Sam.

"I want to hire you to look into these threats on my life, but I know it will take some time. For the immediate future, I'm wondering if you could help me hire someone to stay and look after me. I know this isn't your usual job, but can you recommend someone?"

"You're right; I'm not in the bodyguard business, but I've already thought of someone I can call," Sam said.

"Could you contact them right now, Sam? I'm sorry to be insistent, but I would really like Joseph and Sarah to be able to get out of here tonight or tomorrow morning because the weatherman says we'll be getting a pretty big snowstorm. I don't want them stuck here," Casey insisted.

Her hand shook slightly as she handed him a cell phone, but Sam took it firmly and walked outside for a quieter atmosphere. When he returned to the table, he was smiling. "I can have a very reliable man sometime tomorrow. He's driving in from Philly, but can make it— at the latest—by early afternoon. He's an old buddy of mine, and I'm certain if anyone can keep you safe, he can. I told him I'd call him when I get back to the office with more details. He's a good man, Casey—an ex-cop. I can start looking into these incidents right away, and I promise I'll do what I can to find this person that's after you."

Sam saw the look of relief on both Casey and Joseph's faces.

"I may as well get started right away. Two important questions to think about: Who might want you dead? And what motive could that person possibly have? Mull those two questions over, and call me tomorrow with your thoughts." Sam rose to leave, but Casey's voice stopped him.

"I don't need any more time to think about it—we've already given it a lot of thought," Casey answered, and Sam took his notebook out again. "I believe you might want to start this investigation with a visit to my attorney, Wayne Durham of Durham, Warren, and Smith. Do you know the firm?"

"On Broad Street, right? The one that has a big storefront office and probably more than one working elevator?" Sam joked.

"That's the one," Casey said. "I'll call Mr. Durham and give him permission to share the provisions of my father's will. The answer has to be in that will."

Her statement gave Sam an old familiar itch—a will? An attempted murder? What was really happening here?

CHAPTER TWO

Danny hopped down from the truck bed and followed the others, who formed a line in front of a large man with a bushy head of hair and a fist full of cash.

"I can't thank you enough for getting the roof on my house done before the storm comes. There's an extra ten dollars for each of you," the man said.

Danny stared at the three twenties and the ten the man had counted into his hand. In his twenty-one years, Danny had never made so money in one day. He was tired, grimy and his bones ached from a cold day spent on a roof, but now he knew it had been worth it and that he had been lucky to be chosen for the job.

He could hear Gus' words from long ago: *Nothing fills a belly better than honest work.* He and Gus could have eaten for several weeks with this money, and maybe fit in a stay one night at a hotel for a hot shower. For now, he'd celebrate with a meal at his favorite diner, a place where he knew he could get a home-cooked meal for a few bucks.

As he made the long walk to the restaurant, he couldn't help thinking of his old friend. For the thousandth time, Danny acknowledged in his heart that he would never have survived the last eleven years without Gus, who had taught Danny how to defend himself against those who would take his money, his possessions or his dignity.

Now, as Danny came to the restaurant where he and his friend had eaten so many times, he ached for the companionship they'd had. It had been a long time since Danny had anyone to talk to.

As he sat in the diner, slowly eating a hamburger, Danny watched the people around him. He had filled many a lonely day watching those around him and wondering about their lives. *What would it feel like to go to the same job every day*, Danny thought as he studied a neatly groomed man in a suit. Was it boring or did the man love his work? Danny knew how to work hard when he could find the work, but he never knew what he'd be doing from day to day.

Danny turned to study a mother and two small children at the cash register, the mother holding the bouncing kids in place with one arm while she dug for money in a giant purse. Though he often wished he could have been like those children, confident that their mom would take care of things, would get them to school, would clean up their messes, Danny didn't dwell on what he'd never had. He knew that where he was concerned, he'd been lucky to have found a friend like Gus.

Danny ate the final bite of his hamburger and decided that instead of wasting money on a cup of coffee to break the brisk chill of this long day, he'd order a warm piece of apple pie. Because experience had taught him to always be aware of his surroundings, his eyes wandered as he waited for the pie, and eventually, they strayed to the front window. What he saw raised his hackles. There, resting against a streetlamp, but staring straight at Danny through the window was Butch. Butch and his thugs spent a lot of their time sniffing out someone living on the streets that had come into extra food or money. Butch especially hated Danny because Danny could outrun the gang. They hadn't caught him yet, despite numerous tries.

But Danny finished every bite of his pie before he stood calmly, fished in his backpack for the bills he needed, put a small tip on the table, and went to pay the cashier. He then strolled casually towards the restroom, but on the way, he turned sharply into an adjacent swinging door, throwing out a quick "hello" to his friend Conner, the cook, as he picked up the pace, ran through the kitchen, and out the back door. Danny knew the kitchen and its back alley well because he'd been hired several times by Conner to wash the dishes or peel potatoes in exchange for a meal. Now, Danny headed up the alley toward freedom.

But Butch had learned from previous encounters that Danny had friends in the kitchen. Two of the thugs were just coming around the corner of the building when Danny came out of the alley way—and the race was on. Danny took off in the opposite direction, his feet pummeling the pavement, his leg muscles working their magic. He kept to the streets he knew well, those with few pedestrians to run into and alleys that didn't dead end. Behind him came shouts of derision, then Danny heard a dull thud and felt a sharp pain at the back of his head. He realized one of the thugs had stopped long enough to pick up a rock or brick and had good enough aim to hit the running target. Danny felt the hot trickle of blood creep down his neck, but he knew better than to stop. He knew this was not just a race of speed, but of endurance. He could feel the rapid pumping of his own blood as his lungs filled with the now-frigid air, but he knew the two guys after him wouldn't exert much effort, not knowing exactly what they'd get from the ordeal.

Yet it took almost ten minutes of running until the shouts began to subside. Eventually, he heard nothing, so he slowed his pace, took deep breaths, and sat in a doorway to rest his muscles. He patted the front pocket of his backpack, seeking the comfort of his wages, and began to think about the next obstacle of the day—where to spend what he knew would be a cold night. Small flurries were already coming down, and he remembered the bushy man's desire to get the job done "before the big storm." A peek in the discarded morning newspaper had shown that D.C. was about to go through one its rare snowstorms. He had extra clothes in the backpack that never left his back, but he knew he needed a place out of the elements. It was too late, and he was too far to go to the ninth street mission where he occasionally slept, and he wasn't willing to spend his wages on a hotel until he either had to or he knew he could replace them.

In the distance, Danny heard the whistle of a train. "That's it," he thought, as he headed in the direction of the train tracks. He had used one particular night-time place a few times before when he needed to get out of the elements—an empty railroad car in an area that was usually abandoned. Within minutes he found the car and crawled inside, where he found the piles of hay he knew would be there. Wearily, he sprawled on top of the piles and covered his body with more of the sweet smelling hay.

He fell into a deep sleep, glad he'd been able to use his muscles that day both to make money and keep himself safe from others, and peaceful in the knowledge he'd eat the next day.

CHAPTER THREE

As Sam headed back to his office, Casey's words were playing in his head. "It's all in the will," whispered through his mind. Sam liked very few things more than a puzzle. He had been that way since he was a child, and it was one of the main reasons he had become a detective. He paced the office floor, then grabbed his overcoat and headed back out the door, turning his car in the direction of the offices of Durham, Warren, and Smith.

The friendly receptionist did not even question whether Sam had an appointment when he mentioned he was there on behalf of Cassandra Lewis.

Wayne Durham's slightly graying hair topped a tall lean body. He extended a hand towards Sam, a pleasant smile on his face.

"It's good of you to meet me on short notice," Sam said as he grasped the other man's hand. "Casey said she'd call and let you know I was coming."

"She called me not five minutes ago," the lawyer said. "And I couldn't be more pleased. She seems quite concerned about what is happening and not convinced the police can do anything, so I'm glad to see she's hired outside help. Please sit down." Durham poured a cup of tea from an expensive tea set atop the marble-topped coffee table. Instead of a desk environment, Wayne and Sam were seated in a comfortable alcove with love seat and arm chair.

"Tea?" Wayne said.

"No thank you," Sam replied, opening his notebook and taking a pen from his pocket. "Casey mentioned her father's will to me earlier today—"

"Ah, yes, the infamous will," Wayne sighed. "To this day, I have no idea what Richard was up to, and I tried to talk him out of changing the will so drastically, but to no avail. You see, it was just two weeks before his death that Richard called me in to make various changes."

"Did he give a reason for the changes?" Sam asked.

"I don't generally ask my clients for reasons, Mr. Osborne. But he seemed a little edgy that day, as if he were angry or worried. Normally, Richard was a calm, though forceful man—he usually knew exactly what he wanted. But that day he was just anxious to get on with it."

"And he never mentioned any impending trouble or anxieties?"

"No, and I really didn't pursue it very far. I knew Richard well enough not to push him." Wayne rested back against the loveseat then.

"After the accident, I'll admit, the thought occurred to me that he had may have known something was wrong or about to happen." The lawyer rubbed one manicured hand across his eyes.

Sam realized he'd probably gotten the lawyer at the end of a long day. He kept quiet.

Wayne opened his eyes, then, and snapped back into efficiency mode.

"In the original document, Richard left five hundred thousand dollars to his first wife Anna Mae Lewis, who is the mother of Ricky, Richard's son and Casey's half brother. Anna Mae is a minor partner in the pharmaceutical business Richard owned, and the two maintained a business relationship after the divorce.

"Richard also made provisions of one hundred thousand dollars each to John Hutchins, his business manager, and to Reginald Stone, the other minor partner in the business, as well as to Joseph and Sarah Lindquist, his housekeepers, who now live with Casey. The balance of his very sizable estate was to be distributed equally among his second wife, Helen, and the three children living in his household—Casey, Ricky and Casey's other half sister Ginger Johnson. Helen, who is both Casey and Ginger's mother, perished in the same car accident, however. That would have left the estate to his three children if he hadn't made certain changes."

"Ginger Johnson? Is she a married daughter?" Sam looked up from his notes.

"Johnson is Helen's first husband's name. Richard helped raise Ginger, and she lived with the family for much of her life, which is why she was part of the original will, I guess."

The lawyer rose then and began to pace, his body tense, his hands behind his back.

"The new will changed things drastically, however," he said. "In it, he left the bulk of his estate to his second wife, Helen, with fifty thousand dollars per year in trust funds for Casey, Ricky, Ginger, and Anna Mae. Casey will inherit the rest of her half of the estate when she turns twenty one."

Wayne sat down again and picked up his tea cup.

"But that's not the only strange part. Richard also put into the new will that on Casey's twenty-first birthday, the fifty thousand dollars in annually distributed trust funds for the other three—Anna Mae, Ricky and Ginger—were to cease. Helen, if she'd lived, and Casey would have split what remained of the estate. And Casey was to get control of Richard's company."

"And the other parties named in the will?"

"Nothing was left to either John Hutchins or Reginald Stone, though the Lindquists were still given one hundred thousand," Wayne said.

"And what did the will say would happen if Casey and Helen were to pass away?"

"I don't think he even considered that, and it wasn't specified in the will. She was only thirteen at the time," Wayne said with a sigh. "Ginger inherited about one hundred thousand dollars from a separate will made out by Helen. But Richard clearly intended for Casey and Helen to inherit and for Casey to take over the company—she gained control of the majority shares in the stock portfolio, and he specified she could do what she wanted with it."

"Even though she was only thirteen at the time?" Sam asked.

"He took her youth into consideration by specifying that the company was to continue under John Hutchins's management and Reginald Stone and Anna Mae's control, until Cassandra's twenty-first birthday," Wayne leaned back in his chair to regard Sam. He steepled his fingers, "At that time, there would be a complete audit of the books, then Casey could decide to keep the stock, sell it, buy their shares, run the company, whatever she wanted.

"You can see what a big change the new will made—cutting Ricky, Ginger, and Anna Mae's inheritances substantially so that the most they'd get was a total of fifty thousand dollars each over the seven years, and knocking Hutchins and Stone out completely—I guess figuring they would make money while the company made money," said the lawyer.

Sam leafed through his notes. "So, Ricky, Ginger, and the first wife will receive no more money once Casey turns twenty one?" Sam frowned at this point and ran his pen tip over his notes. Finally he turned a page in the notebook, looked at the lawyer and asked, "How much was Richard Lewis worth?"

"At the time of his death, about eight million; Today, approximately twelve million—

the company seems to be doing well under the management of John Hutchins, Reginald Stone, and Anna Mae Lewis' control," Durham said.

Sam leaned forward then and asked, "And what would happen to the inheritance if Casey is out of the scene?"

"The will would go into probate, but I believe the estate goes to the next of kin, which would be Ricky. Anna Mae and Ginger could contest that, but I believe he'd inherit the whole of it. The other two aren't blood relatives. Casey has scheduled to make out her own will once she turns twenty-one and inherits."

"You said he didn't give you any reason for the changes at the time? Do you have any ideas about it now?"

"I heard rumors after Richard's death, but they were only rumors," Wayne said, rising as if to dismiss Sam.

But Sam didn't take the bait.

"I know you don't want to spread gossip, Mr. Durham. But sometimes rumors contain half truths," Sam said, not looking up from his notes. "If you truly want to help Casey, who is *your* client, please share with me the general feelings of what was going on."

Wayne sat back down, paused, and then looked at Sam.

"Ginger and Ricky were wild teenagers, and Richard had to bail them out of trouble many times. The two were always very close and got into a lot of scrapes together. He may have just got fed up with that scenario and their irresponsibility. That could very well explain the—" Wayne's right hand came up from his lap to stroke his chin as he sought the right word, "*disenchantment* that eventually developed. As far as Anna Mae, though they kept up a friendly façade, the feeling is that they were constantly at odds over business decisions. I was surprised, frankly, that he left her so much money in the original will. As for the other two—Reggie Johnson and John Hutchins—he may have just been trying to ensure they kept the business healthy."

"About the accident that killed Richard and Helen: is there any reason to believe the crash was anything other than an accident?" Sam asked.

"The police ruled Richard to be at fault. They had been at a party that night; the report concluded that he drank too much and took a corner too quickly." Wayne looked away from Sam then, out the office window.

"I do know that Casey doesn't believe the accident was caused by the alcohol," Wayne said. He turned back to Sam and rose again. This time, Sam knew the interview was over.

"Ask her about it when you get a chance," Durham paused at the door to show Sam out.

Sam shook the lawyer's hand and left the office. His mind was so wrapped around thoughts and details of what could have happened, he didn't notice the snow was falling harder than when he had arrived.

"I think I have my work cut out for me with this one," he muttered to himself as he reached his car only to find it covered with an inch of the cold white powder.

CHAPTER FOUR

Danny awoke early the next morning with a start when he heard a whistle blow. He felt a sudden jerk of the car around him, and then another. *God, was it possible? Was the train really moving?*

Danny lay there in the hay for several minutes, not fully awake, his head aching from last night's run-in with Butch's thugs. He touched his head where the rock had hit him. The dried blood had formed a six-inch patch across the back of his head, and the area around it was sore.

He sat up suddenly, remembering the jerk of the train and feeling movement. The gray metal walls and mounds of hay swirled before his eyes, and Danny laid his head against his drawn up knees for several minutes, willing the dizziness to go away.

When he felt steadier, Danny rose and went to the railcar door. He pushed the heavy door open and gazed out at a landscape completely covered with layers of snow. The train wasn't moving fast, but it was fast enough that Danny was hesitant to jump. He knew what a broken bone could do to someone wandering the streets, especially in the cold, and his head still hurt. Besides, he had no place he had to be.

He stood for a moment gazing out at snow-covered fields with his legs dangling out the car. "Where am I?" Danny asked aloud, although he knew the train couldn't be far from the city. Snow meant harsh days ahead for someone without a permanent roof, but he couldn't help admiring what it could do to create a different perspective on the world. There were still a few houses on the horizon, but most of what he could see was a blank slate of white, unspoiled by cars or pedestrians or even animals.

The cold eventually seeped inside the clothes he'd worn yesterday before the snow had begun, so he withdrew from the doorway and shut the frozen world out. He pulled his backpack close and sat down on an untied bale of hay, drawing it to his chest and saying a silent thank you to Gus for advising him to always have his pack nearby. Unzipping the pack, he took out a pair of old rubber boots and put them to the side, smiling at the memory of scoffing at Gus' delight when he found the heavy cast-offs. Danny had been through enough winters now to know how valuable those boots could be.

He then took out a lightweight waterproof jacket and put it on over the thick thermal shirt he was already wearing. He also withdrew a thick woolen scarf that he wound around his mouth and nose.

Danny could hear Gus' words in his head. "The scarf will keep your head, your neck, and your ears warm, and your hands safe if you must break a window to get out of the cold."

Danny then withdrew a pair of heavy blue jeans to replace the lighter-weight khakis he wore, took off the khakis and put the jeans on over the long-johns he already had on. With woolen socks and the rubber boots completing his armor against the elements, he neatly folded his old khakis and placed them inside the pack.

Deciding he wasn't going anywhere for awhile, Danny burrowed back down into the hay, grateful for its warmth and not caring about the lingering odor of the farm animals the car had once transported. His head still ached, but at least he would not freeze to death in this place. He turned over and tried to sleep.

After many hours of slipping into and out of sleep, Danny felt the train slow. *We must be approaching a town.* He rolled over, arose slowly and brushed the hay from his clothes, then opened the railcar door again. His teeth chattered softly as he felt the chill.

Allentown, Pennsylvania, Danny read on a passing billboard as the train slowed further. Although still leery of injury, he needed to jump before the trained pulled into a rail yard and someone noticed his presence.

Taking a gulp of air, Danny shut his eyes for a moment, then opened them and leaped toward a snowy embankment. His choice of place to land was a good one, leaving him mostly unscathed, though his head pounded some. Danny got up, shook the snow from his clothes and looked around. He was a few dozen yards from the train yard, and he could see the road leading up to it. The road was populated by a gas station and a truck stop, along with several commuter parking lots, which appeared to be mostly empty. Off in the distance, a four-lane road stretched parallel to the train station's access road. Danny brushed off his pack and put it on, then headed toward the gas station.

He needed the warmth of a building that was heated.

At the gas station, Danny bought a cup of coffee to warm his insides, as well as a pack of donuts to fill the ache that a half day without food had created in his belly. He looked around the station, noting that he was the only person there at the moment and that the clerk behind the counter was paying him no heed, caught up as the pimply teen was in the latest issue of *American Curves* magazine.

Danny knew he needed to find a way back to D.C., but he didn't want to spend his hard-earned dollars on a rail ticket if he could help it—it would probably take most of what he had. Maybe he could hitch a ride, but if that were the case, he'd need more protection. Danny purchased a pair of inexpensive, but thick cotton gloves probably meant for garden work, as well as a stocking cap. They'd at least keep his hands and ears warm. He also bought a bottle of water and a few boiled eggs because they were on sale two for one and would provide a good source of sticking-power food. He ventured out, then, to assess the road situation.

What he found did not give him much hope. The four-lane road looked like a state highway, but the weather had slowed traffic considerably.

Only a few cars were traveling cautiously down the route. Still, he was bound to get a lift eventually, and it was close enough to the gas station that if he needed to return for warmth he could do so.

However, Danny was only to the edge of the parking lot when a semi truck coming out of the truck stop across the road slowed beside him. The driver rolled down the window and yelled, "Going somewhere young man? It's awful nasty out here."

"Well, sir. I'm heading south," Danny said, his mind working to prepare a story. But the truck driver asked no further questions before he said, "I could get you to just east of Harrisonburg, Pennsylvania, where I get on the turnpike."

Danny didn't hesitate. He ran around to the other side and got into a warm cab.

"Anywhere heading south is fine, Sir. I'm sure I can get a ride at the turnpike. Thanks for picking me up."

"No one should be out in this weather. What possessed you to be standing all alone out there?" the driver asked.

Danny's answer came easily. "My grandma lives in York, and she's sick, but my car gave out on me. It's in the gas station's repair bay, but they can't work on it until the next day or so. I really need to get to her. I'm not sure she's going to make it."

"Well settle back and I'll get ya a chunk of the way there," the driver said, his craggy face breaking into a grin. "You can call someone to pick you up at the exit." He turned up the country western music station and turned his eyes back to the road.

Danny secretly thanked his guardian angel Gus for the warmth of the cab. The scraping of the windshield and the music lulled Danny to sleep.

"Sorry," the truck driver's voice cut through Danny's nap as he shook Danny's arm lightly, "We're here at the turnpike exit where I have to turn off. Time to get out."

Danny thanked the man again, and jumped down into snow halfway up to his knees. *Oh boy, the going will be much rougher now.*

He said another silent "thanks" for the boots on his feet, the warmth of his thermal shirt and the waterproof jacket. The snow lay in heavy layers, the surface swirling from a wind that had picked up. Looking around him, Danny could see snow plows hadn't yet caught up to the worsening roads. He made sure the trucker had driven off, and then set out to find anything open close to the exit where he might find shelter.

Luck was with him again. He had hiked only a short distance when a pickup truck slowed, its window rolled down, and the face of an elderly man emerged.

"Son, what the hell are you DOING out her in the damn snow!" the man's gravelly voice boomed out.

Danny repeated his grandma story, adding that a cousin would be picking him up outside York.

"You still shouldn't be out in this weather, young man, but I'll be glad to get you a bit further. I'm going about forty miles down the road, and you're welcome to ride along," the older man said.

Grinning broadly, Danny didn't hesitate. He trudged around the front of the truck, opened the passenger door, and then carefully knocked the snow off his boots and clothes before climbing inside.

The cab wasn't quite as warm as the semi, but the driver was much more vocal than the semi's driver had been. The two chatted easily, the old man filling Danny in on his 10 grandkids and the fact he was "still married to the gal I courted in high school." Danny relaxed into telling a tale about a construction company job, a girlfriend back home, and a childhood filled with memories of the grandma he was trying to reach.

Before long, the forty miles were behind them, and the elderly gentleman was slowing at an intersection and pulling into a lot, explaining that the town of Lancaster was just ahead on this road.

"Looks like Cooger's bar is still open. You can call your cousin from here," the old man said, motioning at the brightly lit building at the end of the parking lot. "I got to turn off and get home to Bertha before I can't."

Danny thanked the man again, and got out of the truck. The lot had been plowed, though it must have been a while ago, but the walking was easy to the door of the bar. However, when he got to the door, he discovered the old man had been wrong. Although the outside light was still on, no one came to the door, despite Danny's repeated pounding.

Danny knew he was in trouble. He looked around through the heavy, blowing snow and walked to the end of the lot, gazing up the road. He couldn't see very far, but he saw the glow of lights just down the road.

He looked back at the bar and considered briefly breaking in. He had the tools in his pack or he could use his fist. But he really had no idea how long the snow would last, if the bar really had the alarm the sticker on the door proclaimed, or how far he was from a police station that would respond should a break-in occur.

He decided he had no choice; he'd head for the lights.

As if divine forces approved of his decision, the wind suddenly let up, though the snow remained heavy. Danny set off down the road.

This isn't so bad. The cold is not so bad. You looking out for me again, Gus?

But after ten minutes, he knew that part of the reason he wasn't feeling the cold was that it had seeped too far into his clothes and his bones. The wind had picked up again, and the bitter chill was making him groggy. He could barely see in front of him now, and he'd lost sight of the lights. Had he taken a wrong turn? Was he still on the road? His usual optimism began to falter, frozen more with each gust. But he trudged on, driven forward by mental conversations with Gus, with the old man in the truck, even with the truck driver. Driven on by memories of other times he'd faced danger and won. Driven on by books he'd read whose plots he recalled in vivid detail. He needed to keep his mind active to keep his body moving forward.

Danny stood still for a moment in the cold, the wind whipping the ends of his scarf, trying to get his bearings. He thought he saw the lights again and headed towards the outline of a building. When he was about half a football field from the building, however, the glow disappeared. He was gasping for air when he reached the door and pounded heavily on it.

No one answered his plea. Whoever had been there and whatever the building was, it was now just an empty, closed building with a metal door and a lock too heavy and large for him to pick.

Danny knew he was in trouble if he couldn't find some place to get out of the wind and the moisture. Was this how his life would end— not in an alley with bruises from a beating, but in the middle of Pennsylvania, frozen by the elements?

No, it will not. He took a moment to pull the scarf up over his nose again and feel the warmth of his own breath. Then he turned and trudged on through the blinding snow.

CHAPTER FIVE

Casey pulled back the curtain and peered out at the light flutter of snow that had been falling all day. At first, it had melted quickly, but now it was sticking to the grass and beginning to pile up.

"Joseph," she called, "could you and Sarah come in here, please?" She let the curtain fall back across the window.

Joseph came into the living room with Sarah in tow. They both rushed to Casey's side, and Joseph took Casey's hand. "What's wrong, Casey? Are you feeling all right?"

"I'm fine, Joseph," Casey said with a soft laugh. She didn't often "summon" anyone into a room. The three of them had become a family unit, moving smoothly within the confines of their routines, but sharing much more than living arrangements.

Casey had glimpsed the magnitude of the snowstorm, and it had her worried.

"They're predicting a huge storm tonight," she said. "I want you to leave for Lucy's immediately. You need to get on the road before it gets bad."

"We'll leave in the morning as planned," Joseph said and turned back to the room he'd left.

Sarah hesitated, however. "I'm certain the storm won't be as bad as the weatherman says. You know they're usually wrong."

Joseph turned back then, glancing first at his wife, then at Casey. "We won't leave you until the bodyguard comes," he said firmly, "and perhaps we should postpone the trip."

Casey glimpsed the emotion that ran across Sarah's face. Sarah's sister was scheduled for heart surgery in two days. Casey knew Sarah just wanted to be at her sister's side.

Casey rolled forward to take Sarah's hand. "No. I have to insist. Take the four-wheel drive and leave here as soon as you can get packed. I couldn't stand it if anything should happen to you. Lucy needs you." She reached into her pocket and withdrew the car keys.

Sarah and Joseph exchanged a look, but neither took the keys. They turned to face the girl they'd cared for most of her life.

"You might need us. Especially if the snow is bad—" Sarah began.

Casey rolled back from the couple then and gave them what she hoped was a convincing glare. Her eyebrows raised and she tapped the finger of one hand against the chair handle. The other still held the keys.

"You know I can get by for a short time, and the bodyguard will be available to help starting tomorrow," she said. "I have my cell phone, and I'll call for help if anything comes up. If I know Sarah, she's already cooked up enough food for a decade and left it in the fridge." Casey's face softened then. She could never really be angry with these two.

"It's time to stop worrying about me and start worrying about Lucy. I'll lock all the doors behind you. But please get ready and go now."

Sarah and Joseph exchanged another look, but smiled. They turned back to Casey and Joseph held out his hand. Casey dropped the keys into his hand, and the couple went to pack.

An hour and half later, they each planted a kiss on Casey's cheek and, having run down a long list of dos and do-nots, left Casey to herself.

Casey rolled through the house, the sound of her wheels on hardwood floors echoing. The sound wasn't a lonely one for Casey, however. It wasn't often that Joseph and Sarah were both gone, and she savored the feeling of quiet, eventually settling in the spacious sitting room with a good book in front of a fire Joseph had left in the grate.

The feeling didn't last long.

The first knock at the door came from her father's business partner, Uncle Reggie, who lived nearby and visited periodically to check on her. Casey met him at the door.

Casey called Reginald "Uncle" not because he was related by blood, but simply because he was a steady fixture in the Lewis house and had been since as long as she could remember. At one time, her father and mother and the Stones had been close friends.

The front door creaked as Reggie shut it behind him. Shaking snowflakes from his long coat, he smoothed it with his hand and hung it on the nearby coat rack. "Getting nasty out there," he said. "I thought I better come check on you before the big storm hits."

He looked around the hallway and peered into nearby rooms, a puzzled look crossing his face. "Where are Joseph and Sarah?"

"I made them leave early so they could get to Lucy's before it gets really bad, but they left me with everything I need."

Casey looked at the wrinkled brow of Uncle Reggie's face and decided to try a little white lie. "Besides, I have a nurse attendant coming first thing in the morning."

Uncle Reggie didn't need to know the man coming was actually a bodyguard, not a nurse, and not scheduled to arrive until the afternoon. "There was no need for you to come out in this weather when I'm sure Ellie needs you at home."

Reggie's wife Ellie was mostly bed ridden; her body racked with the consequences of advanced multiple sclerosis. She was left dependent on Reggie for most everything from the disease, which flared up often. Casey knew Uncle Reggie's visits were sometimes just a reason to be out of his own home. In nice weather, he usually walked.

"You're all alone then?" he said. "Do you want to come and spend the night with Ellie and me?"

Casey smiled at the thought of the short, round Reginald trying to carry her across snowy fields to his own home, though she imagined he'd probably driven the distance tonight. But the thought of a night in Ellie's presence turned the smile into a frown. The disease had sickened Ellie's disposition, as well as her body.

"I'm a big girl, Uncle Reg. I have everything I need, and you're close by. Please don't worry about me. You and Uncle John made certain a long time ago that this house has all the necessary things a girl in a wheelchair needs to get by and the fridge is stocked." She smiled, hoping to reassure him, but Reggie didn't smile back.

"Well, if you're certain," he said, "Can I do anything for you then, before I get back to Ellie?" But he turned and grabbed his coat. He hadn't taken off his boots.

"No, Uncle Reg, I'm fine," she said, and Reggie gave her a little peck on the cheek. He was out the door less than three minutes after he arrived, and Casey sighed in relief.

She rolled back to the sitting room, grabbed a poker, and got the fire going before it could die completely. She knew she'd have to put it out soon, but for now, it added atmosphere to her feeling of peace. She picked up her book and read another chapter, but her peacefulness was short lived.

Another knock at the door and Casey was back at the front hall to watch Ricky and his mother Anna Mae bustle through the door, bringing snow and a chilly breeze with them.

"Hey there little sister, what's rollin'?" Ricky joked as he followed Casey to the living room. Casey glanced at the ceiling and grimaced, but she knew Ricky wouldn't even notice.

Casey settled her expression into what she hoped was pleasant and asked, "What brings you two out in this weather?"

"We're just concerned about you, dear. It's beginning to really come down out there, and we heard you were all alone," Anna Mae said. She carefully removed her expensive leather gloves and laid them on a nearby sofa arm. Then she settled her trim but shapely body on the sofa, smoothing her skirt and tugging at her suit jacket. Despite the snow, Anna Mae was as immaculately dressed as ever.

"Uncle Reggie called us a little while ago," Ricky explained.

Casey sighed. She had suspected Reggie would call the two, and that he'd probably called John Hutchins as well. The four were her designated watch keepers, visiting sporadically to check up on her. She would be grateful for the show of concern if she didn't feel it was connected somehow to her father, the company, and the estate. Sometimes, she felt like they talked among themselves about how best to deal with the orphan soon to hold all the purse strings.

Casey knew she had to assure them she needed no help to get rid of them, so she tested the lie out again.

"I hired a nurse. He'll be here first thing in the morning." The lie tasted just fine on her tongue and was much easier than it had been with Uncle Reggie. They didn't need to know the extent of her fears or the fact the hired help was a bodyguard. She'd told them of the incidents that she thought were attempts on her life, but not the depth of her fears. All four watch keepers had pretty much dismissed what happened as the imaginings of a girl with a lot of time on her hands.

"Joseph and Sarah intended to leave in the morning," Casey explained to Anna Mae and Ricky, "but I made them leave early so they could get to Dumfries before the storm really comes," Casey explained.

"Guess that was smart to get 'em on the road," Ricky acknowledged as he looked around. Casey knew he was trying to locate the decanter of whiskey that was usually present for company. She tried a pre-emptive roll toward the door, "And you two should be on your way as well. It's really coming down out there now, and you should get home before it gets bad."

The pre-emptive move failed miserably as Ricky made contact with the decanter and a glass. He poured two short drinks, handing the second glass to Anna Mae.

"A male nurse, Casey?" Anna Mae asked, her gaze wandering the room and settling on the oil painting of Richard over the fireplace. "Won't that look strange to people in town? Is he going to live here at the house with you? Will you be alone with this man until Joseph and Sarah return?"

"A male nurse will be better able to lift me when it's necessary," Casey replied in an even tone. But she couldn't help adding, "I'm certain my virginity is safe, Anna Mae. There are some advantages to this handicap."

A look of distaste crossed Anna Mae's well-tended facial features, but she raised a manicured hand, took a sip of the whiskey, and set the glass on a nearby table.

"I guess it will be all right," Anna Mae said, as if granting Casey permission. "I don't suppose you'll tempt him much."

Casey flinched inwardly, but her face was frozen into a smile. She had long ago given up on getting support or understanding from this woman who added tension to any gathering of family and friends. Casey had developed the skill of letting Anna Mae's comments wash over her while making small talk long enough to get Anna Mae out of a room.

After a few more trivial exchanges about the weather, what was happening with the company, and another snootful of whiskey on Ricky's part, Anna Mae rose, turned to Casey and asked, "Is there anything I can get for you, dear, before Ricky and I leave?"

"No, I appreciate it, but I'm set for the evening—just about to grab a glass of water and go to bed with my book for a couple hours," Casey said, turning her chair, book on lap, towards the door again to emphasize her words.

"Oh, well let me get that water for you—" Anna Mae hopped up and moved toward the kitchen before Casey could stop her. Gritting her teeth, she said a quick "thanks" when Anna Mae returned with a full glass of water.

Ricky held his mother's coat in his hands, as they finally prepared to leave. "Why don't you call Ginger? She might come and stay with you if you'd just pick up the phone and call her," he said.

"I don't need company. I've got my book. I'm fine by myself," Casey insisted. "And I have my cell phone."

"Guess we have no worries then. Let's go, Mom."

Casey stared at the door for a few minutes after they'd left, feeling the softly percolating anger that always accompanied a visit from Anna Mae. The woman had been around Casey enough to know that getting her a glass of water was more insult than aid. Although Casey spent too many years after the accident feeling sorry for herself and letting Joseph and Sarah wait on her every need, which was a long time ago. And calling Ginger? Ricky knew better than that. Casey had no desire to call her half-sister. As a teen, the older girl had been an idol for the young Casey, who sat for hours watching Ginger carefully apply mascara or put together outfits from piles of clothes tossed on a bed. However, since the accident, Casey and Ginger had very little contact. Ever since Richard's new will was announced, Ginger had been cold and had visited or called only a handful of times over the years. Casey knew Ricky hadn't been too happy about the will either, but, for whatever reasons, he made an attempt to stay friendly, and kept trying to get the two girls together.

Casey wore a scowl now as she wheeled through the house, checking to make sure every door and window was locked. No, she would not call Ginger.

By the time she headed to kitchen to fulfill her promise to Sarah to eat dinner, the scowl was gone, the book again on her lap. But she hadn't even opened it, much less warmed up her dinner before "Uncle" John knocked.

Unlike Reggie, Casey didn't call John Hutchins "uncle" to his face, though others often attached that title when talking to Casey about the man who had been her father's business manager. John had acted as Casey's financial manager and legal adviser in the early days after the accident as the company reeled from losing its chief executive. And though she'd long since gotten her own lawyer and accountant, Casey valued his professional opinion, but she didn't particularly relish his company.

Casey opened the door, and John strolled in, leaning over to give Casey his usual cold kiss on the forehead. His tall, lean frame had to bend low to accomplish the task. When he straightened, Casey peered up at the aquiline nose and thin lips she had come to know well from that angle.

"I hear you are all alone for the night," John said, as he brushed snowflakes from his overcoat.

"Uncle Reggie called?" Casey said with a sigh.

"No, Anna Mae called me," he said as he turned, surveying the empty hallway. "It should have been you. Left all alone here without Sarah and Joseph. Are you sure that's wise?"

Casey sighed again. *Why was she always explaining that she could take care of herself?* "I didn't think it necessary to call you," she said. "It all came about very fast, with the snow and the Lindquists leaving early. And it's really no big deal, Uncle John. I hired a nurse. He'll be here first thing in the morning. I am perfectly safe for one night."

"Well, I know that," he bristled. "I know you take care of yourself just fine. But it is a long time until morning. You should have someone here. Do you want me to stay?"

Casey shook her head firmly, her blond hair swinging from side to side. "John, I appreciate you looking in on me, but I was just about to eat dinner. Then I intend to retire for the evening, and by morning I'll have someone else here. I have my cell. My fridge is stocked. I'll be fine. Why don't you get back to your place before the snow gets worse?"

"Okay, Casey. I'll call you in a day or so. We have to talk about setting up the audit," John said, as he pulled out his electronic notebook. He took out the stylus attached to the pad and noted something on the device.

Casey knew she was being impolite, but she was tired of sharing her alone moments with others.

"Great. I'll get back to my meal, and you can be on your way."

John looked up then and caught her gaze. His steely gray eyes appeared to widen, but Casey didn't really care if she'd insulted him.

"Yes. On my way then, Casey dear. I'll leave you to your dinner. But I'll check with you on a schedule for the audit after the plows get through tomorrow." And then, in less time than it had taken for Reggie's visit, he was on his way out the door.

At least he didn't ask me to call Ginger, Casey thought.

She turned and retreated to the kitchen, opened the refrigerator and withdrew one of the many marked casseroles, read the instructions, and plopped the evening's meal in the microwave.

Alone at last at the kitchen table with her book, she took a few bites of the meal Sarah had prepared, and then shoved her plate away. As often happened with a good book, Casey forgot the visitors who came to her, forgot the snow, forgot Sarah and Joseph's woes, and entered the world a writer had created for her. There would be no one else to disrupt her peace that night.

CHAPTER SIX

Reginald Stone's head was bent into the wind, his gloved hands deep in his pockets for double protection, his stride steady. He opened the door of the house, shook off the snow from his coat, and bent down to take off his calf-high boots. Lifting his head, he looked around at the carefully decorated furnishings—the home could have been snatched off its foundation, transported in time from a country estate and plopped down here on the outskirts of town, except for the fact that the antiques were costly, the curtains made by an interior designer, the plain, solid oak furniture without a flaw in its wood.

Reggie sighed deeply and took off his gloves, laying them carefully on a tall entryway armoire.

A shrill voice came from an adjacent room, "Reggie, is that you? Why have you left me all alone?"

Reggie's footsteps were slow, and his whole body sagged as he made the trip from hallway to living room. A thin woman sat in a wheelchair, her hands twisted at an awkward angle, her face screwed up in a scowl. But Reggie bent down and kissed the woman on her bony cheek.

"I told you, Ellie. I went to see if Cassandra needed anything. There's a big storm brewing outside, and I knew Joseph and Sarah were going on a trip. They actually left early and—"

But he didn't get a chance to finish his explanation.

"You left me for *her*?" Ellie cried, her voice high and full of accusation. "You left me all alone in this snow while you went to check on *her*. She's not even really your niece. I could have needed you!"

"I'm sorry, dear," Reggie apologized, but the words sounded flat, as if he had said them many times.

Reggie sat down on a nearby couch, his gaze settling on the woman as if he was trying to conjure up a different picture than the Ellie whose limp strands of hair hung about her neck, uncombed and greasy. Her skin was sallow, her expression waxen under layers of caked make-up. But still Reggie gazed at her, his head tilted slightly.

"Stop staring at me," she complained. "You left me without food."

"I'm sorry," he said again. "I forgot you had not eaten."

He rose to his feet then and walked woodenly towards the kitchen. Ellie's chair trailed him, its motor humming softly.

"Don't make me another sandwich. I'm tired of sandwiches."

Reggie opened the refrigerator, reached in for the carton of milk, then turned to a cabinet, selected a glass and poured. He held the glass out towards Ellie, and when she did not take it, put it to her mouth. Her eyes closed, she drank deeply. The milk spilled slightly down the front of her bathrobe, joining other food stains.

"Go back to the living room, dear. I'll fix your tray. I'll surprise you the way I used to when I made breakfast in bed on Sundays."

Ellie looked up at him then, her eyebrows raised slightly. But the scowl returned to her brow as she turned and maneuvered her chair out of the room.

Reggie sighed again and turned back to the fridge. He took out some eggs and cheese, shredded the cheese, added a small amount of butter to a frying pan, and poured the whipped eggs into it. His mind seemed to be miles away from what his hands were doing, yet eventually a fluffy golden omelet formed in the pan. For a moment, Reggie seemed to snap back into focus. He gazed at the omelet for several moments, then tilted his head as if he'd come to a decision. He laid the spatula he was holding on the counter, turned to a cupboard, and withdrew a flowered plate and a rosebud vase. He went to another cupboard and drew out a tray. He walked out the back of the kitchen to a greenhouse and came back with a single rose. Placing the rose in the vase, he put the plate, the vase, the omelet, and a single piece of toast on the tray, then carried it to his wife.

Ellie's eyes widened noticeably as Reggie arranged the tray on her lap. She looked up at him for just a moment, before picking up the fork and cutting into the omelet. The omelet soon became an eggy mess on the plate as her fork attempted to make contact with her food. Only a few mouthfuls made it into her mouth, before she pushed the plate away and turned to Reggie.

"I'm tired. Can you help me into bed?"

When Reggie came back downstairs, he picked up the messy plate and the fork and ate the now-cold eggs as he walked back into the kitchen. He left the plate and fork in the sink and returned to the living room, selecting an overstuffed chair in the far corner of the room, the only piece of furniture that looked worn.

The chair sat in its own little alcove, where Reggie could gaze out the bay window. He rubbed his tired-looking eyes and seemed to drift off to sleep.

A half an hour later, Reggie's eyes flew open. He rose from his chair and went out to the garage. There sat an SUV expensively transformed to accommodate an electric chair. Alongside the SUV was a shiny, clean Lexus. Reggie ran his hand along a bumper, a small smile coming to his lips. But his eyes traveled behind the Lexus to fall on the red snowmobile also stored in the oversized garage.

As the wind blew fiercely outside, Reggie took action. He scoured about in a drawer in a garage storage unit until he located a ring with a single fat key. Then he rummaged through boxes stored on the shelves around the garage until he found snowmobile gear. His face suddenly looked alive, younger somehow, and full of excitement. He dressed quickly, raised the garage door, and went out into the cold wearing the gear and a smile.

CHAPTER SEVEN

John Hutchins sat behind the wheel of the brand new Jeep Cherokee cursing softly. His expensive leather gloves and $800 overcoat weren't much good in this kind of snow. The vehicle rested at an awkward angle on the wrong side of the road, one wheel up over the curb. The Jeep appeared to be going nowhere for the moment, and oncoming traffic didn't appear to be a problem. The snow had frozen the comings and goings of anyone in the area.

John sat inside, making no move to leave the vehicle. After several minutes, he took off the gloves and ran one hand through his carefully styled hair, which rustled with the gesture, but fell easily back into place. He looked to his left and saw white. The white-covered curb, a white fence that stretched parallel off into the distance, white street lights above his head that had just flicked on as the sun set. He looked to the right and saw more white—farm fields across the road stretched as far as the eye could see in the gathering darkness.

John's gaze returned to the inside of the car, where he looked down at the floor on the passenger's side. He reached over and drew up a brief case, putting it on his lap and opening it. Inside were a notebook computer and a plain, brown day planner. He flipped through the planner, looking for something, using his forefinger to scratch the edge of his scalp several times. The look on his face was puzzlement. Then, apparently finding what he sought, he rested one hand on a page while reaching inside the breast pocket of his immaculately cut overcoat. He withdrew a cell phone. Flipping it open, he started to dial, only to hear a series of beeps and see a screen grow black.

"Damn, damn, damn. Battery."

With a heavy sigh, he reached forward and restarted the Jeep. Putting the car in drive, then reverse, he tried rocking it out of its current situation. But the vehicle simply wasn't going anywhere, and John started to sweat. With a heavy sigh, he reached back into the back seat and withdrew a pair of galoshes, put them on the passenger's seat and pushed his own seat as far back as it would go. He put on the galoshes as well as the gloves, grabbed the windshield scraper in the back seat, and with effort due to the level of snow and the angle of the car, managed to get the driver's side door opened.

The snow covered most of his shins and crept over the top of his galoshes to wet his shoes. John swore again, a little louder this time, and then trudged around the vehicle, assessing its condition. He tried digging at the wheels, but had only the plastic windshield scraper, which didn't do him much good. By the time he got to the passenger door, which was lower by several inches than the driver's door, he seemed to make a decision. He opened the door, got back into his vehicle and, turning it on to keep the motor running, cracked the windows and settled against the seat, his arms crossed, his handsome face scrunched into a scowl.

In the distance, the muffled sound of motor made him cock his head. He peered out into the snow and dark, but saw nothing. But as the sound got louder and louder, he pushed the button that rolled down the passenger window and stuck his head out, seeking the source of the sound. Though he looked up and down the road, he saw nothing. It wasn't until he looked out into the field that he saw a headlight approaching.

"What the hell—"

The blur behind the light began to take form, and John could see a helmet and handlebars, then the figure of the person approaching on a snowmobile.

The vehicle pulled up close to the car and stopped, its rider fiddling with the handlebars until the engine idled.

"Got a problem, John?"

The rider took off the helmet and shook out a full head of raven hair. The hair nearly matched the black helmet and contrasted sharply with the mostly white snowsuit she wore.

"Lord, Anna Mae. What the hell are you doing out here?"

"Taking my baby for a spin," Anna Mae said, caressing the handlebars of the vehicle. "We don't get snow like this very often. Got yourself in a pickle, have you?" Her voice held a note of derision.

"Well, yes. A bit of problem here. It seems I underestimated the extent of this storm. My Jeep seems to be out of commission."

"I'd say," Anna Mae said with a laugh. "You

appear to be on the wrong side of the street, buddy boy."

John's face reddened slightly, but he regained his composure quickly and opened the car door. Anna Mae did not get off her vehicle to offer help as he stepped too quickly into the snow and nearly ended up sitting in it.

"Whoa there, mister. Steady as she goes. Why get out of your vehicle? You expecting me to rescue you?"

John looked slightly shocked by her words.

"You wouldn't leave me here in the snow, would you?"

Anna Mae put the helmet back on without commenting, but gestured to the back of the snowmobile.

John reached back into his car long enough to roll up the windows, turn off the ignition, then grab his keys and gloves. He straightened and carefully put the gloves back on, turned up his collar to cover his ears, grabbed the briefcase from the front seat, and climbed onto the back of the vehicle, shoving the briefcase in the space behind him and Anna Mae. He sat stiffly until the snowmobile jerked into action. Then he grabbed quickly for Anna Mae, put his arms around her waist and turned his face into her collar.

Once the vehicle was steady in its motion, however, John seemed to relax. He even raised his head several times to gaze out at the blinding landscape of black and white, though the biting chill and breeze from the motion didn't allow much peeking.

When driver and passenger arrived in front of his home, John seemed reluctant to leave the snowmobile. Once off, however, he turned to Anna Mae, and raising his voice to ensure she could hear him over the wind, said, "Why don't you come in for a warm drink. Quinsetta makes a very good hot toddy."

Anna Mae pushed the helmet's face mask up, but made no move to get off.

"I don't think so, John. Not tonight. I am not in the mood," she said, her almost-black eyes looking as if they could cut him in two.

"Oh, I didn't mean it that way, Anna Mae. You've made your position quite clear. I'm just grateful for the ride and thought you could use the warming up. And there are some papers for the Donnelly contract I need you to sign. They're in this case. No telling if any of us will be going far tomorrow and this really should get done tonight. I can fax them tomorrow if I can get your signature."

His words must have convinced her, for she sighed, turned off her beloved machine, and dismounted.

As the two approached the house, John put his arm around Anna Mae. She turned to give him another scorching look, then shrugged off the arm and opened the front door. John smiled slightly as he turned back to gaze at the snowmobile.

CHAPTER EIGHT

When Anna Mae arrived home from John Hutchins' house, she left the snowmobile just inside her garage door, turned on the garage light, then shook the layers of snow from her helmet and brushed the white stuff off her snowsuit and hung it on a hook. Her cheeks were bright red circles, but the rest of her face glowed as if the ride had left her feeling like a new woman. She stood for a moment at the garage's door looking out into the snow, a radiant smile on her face.

But the happiness appeared to fade quickly. Anna Mae turned abruptly and strode through the garage, entering her home using the key on a lanyard around her neck. She walked through the modern, sparkling clean kitchen into an Ethan Allen-furnished great room where her son Ricky sat lounging on the overstuffed sofa, his feet stretched along the couch, his face turned towards the gas-burning fireplace.

"I've left the snowmobile in the garage, the keys in the ignition," she said, bringing Ricky's attention around to her face. Ricky jumped up off the couch and went to the bar, where he made Anna Mae a drink to match his own—tall glass, lots of ice, even more scotch, and splash of water.

She took the drink from him with one hand and rested one finger from her other hand lightly on his cheek for a moment. The hand dropped as she said, "You need a shave."

"And you need a comb," Ricky laughed as he pointed to her hair.

Anna Mae frowned as she ran her hand over her locks. But she brushed past Ricky and sat on a one of the stools at the bar, setting her drink on the counter.

Ricky's eyes lost just a little of the twinkle as he sat down next to her.

"Have a good ride? Looks like the snow is coming down hard."

"It is, dear, it is," Anna Mae said with a far off look in her eye.

"I know it's good weather for the snowmobile, but do you think you should really go back out?" she asked her son. "How many drinks have you had? Ginger can ride another day, you know. You really do spoil your step-sister."

"Stop fretting, Mother. I know what I'm doing on a snowmobile. And it's none of your damn business how many drinks I've had or who I go riding with."

But he said that last with the trace of a grin. Ricky rose and downed the rest of his drink before setting it on the bar.

"I'm off, mother. Told Ginger I'd pick her up a half hour ago—where were you, anyway? You missed a good dinner. Peter made beef stroganoff. Left some in the fridge for you, if you're hungry."

"All right dear. Invite Ginger here if you must. I supposed she'll get lonely in that apartment if the weather is as bad as they say. I'll have some dinner while you're gone," Anna Mae said, waving the back of her hand toward her son as if to hurry him along.

Ricky pecked Anna Mae on her cheek and left through the kitchen. His suit, which was usually hanging next to hers in the garage, was already warming in the mudroom.

"See you in an hour or so," he shouted back at Anna Mae.

Anna Mae sipped her drink and shook her hair out of her face, smoothing the top where it had been mussed by the helmet. She got up from the stool and walked to the dining room to stare into the ornate mirror hanging on the wall. What she saw seemed to please her. She turned left and peeked at her profile, then turned right and did the same. She ran her hands down over the thick cotton shirt and insulated stretchy pants, stopping briefly at her flat stomach and trim thighs.

But she sighed a tired sigh. Returning to the kitchen, she picked up her drink and took it into the great room, stretched out on the couch, a Vanity Fair in her lap. She didn't warm up the stroganoff. She didn't really read the magazine—just flipped through the pages, stopping on the slick advertisements featuring models dressed in clothes so costly they were made to look anything but expensive. The wind outside was howling now and causing the trees to brush across the windows. She shivered, though the house was warm, and then fixed herself another stiff drink.

She briefly dozed, the drink untouched on the coffee table. A half hour later, she heard the garage door open. She took her watered down drink and went upstairs to her bedroom.

In the dim light of the garage, it was hard to distinguish that the snowsuits entwined in an embrace were two separate people. The soft blue of one suit seemed weaved into the dark blue of the bulkier suit.

"Ohmygod, Ricky. I'm so hot for you right now, I don't know if I can wait."

"Then don't," growled a deep male voice, and the sound of a zipper cut through the night.

Ginger pulled back then, placing both hands firmly against Ricky's chest.

"Baby, slow down. It's too damn cold in here. We'll freeze our asses off," Ginger said with a firm tone. But it was accompanied by a laugh. "Wouldn't mommy dearest be delighted to know what her little boy was proposing to do in her pristine garage?"

Ricky groaned, but must have realized she was right about the cold. He pulled back and looked at her then, but shook his head and seemed to calm down.

They both began to take off the suits more slowly, stopping for brief kisses on lips and faces, even hands. Ricky lifted up Ginger's lustrous hair and planted a long wet kiss on the back of her neck, then dropped her hair and reached around to grab one of her breasts, his hand now making contact with sweater instead of snowsuit.

"Down boy. You have a nice warm bed upstairs, and an entire night for this," Ginger whispered, turning towards him, her lips close to his ear. "All we have to do is get by your mum and make some excuse to go to bed."

Ricky finished taking off his suit then, hanging both his and Ginger's on hooks next to Anna Mae's. Raising his shoulders briefly, then letting them fall and letting out a long sigh, he took Ginger's hand and prepared to walk into the house. Once inside the door, he dropped her hand, and they both walked forward.

When they saw that the great room was empty, the gas fireplace turned off, the lights on low, they looked at each other and broke out into grins.

"Last one to my room has to get both of us naked," Ricky said, and they both turned towards the stairs and ran.

CHAPTER NINE

With her book resting on the table, Casey chewed, not really tasting the food. She was only eating because she had promised Sarah she'd keep up with meals. Her caregiver had prepared twelve dishes, noting on the container lids how long to microwave the food.

But Casey cared a lot less about eating than what was in the book before her. During the blinding pain of the first years after her parents' deaths, she had learned that one of the only escapes from the hell in her heart was to bury her mind inside the words she read. She was able escape completely, cared for by other people who cooked her meals, kept her on a schedule, cleaned and cared for the house she lived in, and had even planned the details of burying her loved ones.

Now, as she sat at the scratched oak table, picking at the cold food with her fork, she let her mind enter the book completely, savoring the journey of transporting herself into the writer's world with no one to disrupt her journey.

An hour later, Casey pushed away the half-eaten meal, and then carried the dishes via her lap to the lowered sink, scraping the food into the disposal and putting her plate into the dishwasher.

However, after turning off the kitchen light and wheeling herself into her bedroom, she wasn't so pleased with her aloneness. Casey wasn't used to preparing for bed by herself, and it took twice as long to take off her own clothes and carry them to the hamper as it did when Sarah was at her side. When she tried to slip the flannel nightgown over her head, she got tangled in the cloth and almost fell out of her chair. With a shrug of disgust at herself, Casey whispered a silent thanks to Sarah, who made life so much simpler. She knew she was lucky to be able to afford someone to care for her needs, and she was especially lucky that those who did, cared for her with gentleness and love. Pretty surprising given how cold and distant she'd been with her "servants" in the early days following the accident.

Once Casey had lifted herself into bed via the bar and ropes built over her it for that purpose, she lay back, settling her limbs into pillows and allowing her thoughts to drift. She knew she should be more grateful for the things she had that others did not—including the money to pay for a house specially designed to serve her wheelchair as well as caregivers who had turned surrogate parents and the money to occasionally travel. The bitterness of the early years after the accident had finally subsided, but she knew she needed to make more effort to get out into the world. But just as she was starting to explore her options, the attempts on her life had started, creating a cloud of uncertainty.

As she turned out the light, Casey's mind returned to the night of the party before the accident. That weekend had been one of the first times she could remember feeling like she was part of a big family. All of the people in her life had been together—her mother, her father, her half-brother (who spent less and less time with the family since he'd been banned from regular weekend visits), and her half-sister, who for whatever reason, seemed to tolerate her that weekend more than usual.

The Stones, who had always lived close to the Lewises, and "Uncle" John, with his new wife, who Casey really liked but didn't last but a few months as his spouse, as well as several other executives from the company and their wives had been invited to spend the weekend. Casey's father had rented a mansion in the mountains of New Hampshire that had twenty-seven rooms, with a nice theater, a giant game room with an antique mahogany pool table, and a library with thousands of first-editions and other rare books lining the walls. There was a huge, heated swimming pool outside and a lit tennis court. Best of all for Casey was that because Ginger, Ricky and Casey were the only people in attendance under the age of thirty, her half-siblings had included the thirteen-year-old Cassandra in their activities. They had taught her how to play pool and hit a tennis ball. They had even taught her how to play poker. Casey could remember feeling for the first time that, despite the things they had done to her in the past, she truly had an extended family.

"The police said Daddy was drunk, but I know he wasn't," Casey whispered aloud to herself, just as she had many times in the seven years since that night.

But no one had listened to a hysterical teen, who during the months in the hospital, had repeated her conviction many times, then become wrapped up in her own depression and gradually let it go at the same time she was gradually letting her previous life go.

Much had happened in the seven years since that night, and Casey had come to grips with the reality that she'd probably never know exactly what happened—just that she had changed forever. Now, she closed her book, turned out the light, and with a soft sigh, turned her head into her pillow.

Casey was running in a field at the mansion. A huge crowd of people were playing some kind of game, and she was it. Casey could see herself from above in the dream—she was blindfolded and in trouble, headed for a cliff. The Casey from above wanted to call out a warning to the Casey below. But instead, the two Casey's joined together, and she became the blind and running girl, unable to see where she was going, but knowing she had to keep moving. She could hear the people around her laughing; she felt again the power of leg muscles as she ran without knowing where she was going. She knew she was in danger, felt the futility of moving toward the cliff, but knew somehow it was safer to be on the move than to stop. The wind blew on her face, chilling her to the bone. It was dark and so cold. So very cold.

"What was that?" Casey said as she came fully awake. "Who's there?" But there was no answer. She reached for her lamp so she could turn on the light only to touch air. Had she somehow knocked the lamp off during the dream? Why was she so cold?

She pulled herself up to a sitting position and tried to look around the room, her eyes slowly adjusting to the dark. In the dim gray, she saw one of the drapes pulled open. She was certain it had been drawn when she wheeled into the room—she always kept her curtains closed at night. Now, she could just see a small beam of moonlight streaming into the room from the window—the window was open! She could see snow blowing in, a pile already accumulating on the floor. I've got to close that window, she reached for the bar assembly above her bed. It wasn't there. Casey frantically reached around in the dimness, searching for the bar or the chair or anything she could touch, and suddenly she felt a shove—two hands pushing her to the edge of the bed. She tried to turn around to see the person and tell them to stop, but she was falling over the edge. Her head hit the floor; she heard a thundering in her ears. Then the darkness became complete and swallowed her.

Casey awoke with a pounding headache. It was very cold and very dark there on the floor. But why was she lying on the floor? She remembered, then, the hands on her back, and she tried to move, but her arms hurt and her head thumped. She shivered and tried to assess her condition and her surroundings. She saw again the moonlight and the open window, but it was too high up for her to reach. She groaned aloud as she touched around on her upper body and felt something warm. She was bleeding. Her head and one arm had been cut in the fall.

My cell phone, Casey thought. She pulled herself towards the night stand, using her un-scratched arm. Holding tightly to the bottom bed rails with one hand, she stretched towards the top of the table, the pain in her head making her want to scream. But there was no phone, no lamp, nothing on the table.

"I am not going to let someone kill me," she whispered, the words coming out as frozen gusts of breath. Her lungs felt like they were filled with the snow. She dragged her body across the floor using her good arm, trying to reach her bedroom door and stopping to rest when the exertion was too great. The hours it seemed to take to get to that door were, in reality, only ten minutes. And her exertion was rewarded with deep disappointment. She managed to reach the door knob only to discover the door was locked. She was trapped in this room with no way to contact anyone and a raging storm outside.

"I won't die, you son of a bitch," she screamed, her raspy voice breaking through the cold and echoing against the walls in the empty room. "I won't die," she repeated, this time in a whisper. She dragged her body back towards the bed. Once there, she reached up with her bloody arm and tugged at the blanket and comforter repeatedly until they were down on the floor. She rested for a few moments from the effort, and then tackled the next thing she could think to do.

Casey shook the covers as best she could, lying flat on her back. She pushed herself to a sitting position and shook them again, stretching them out over the floor. When she felt she had the covers as good as her pounding head would allow, she dragged her body to the edge of both the blanket and comforter, rolled onto the bedding, then grabbed its edges and rolled inward, turning herself into a cocoon.

For the next few hours, the wind kept blowing snow into the room and the temperature kept dropping. It was a record blizzard for south central Pennsylvania, and while most families were inside their homes, cozy and safe, Cassandra Lewis lay bundled up on her floor with the snow piling up next to the window.

"I will not let you kill me," she said aloud just before she lost consciousness again.

CHAPTER TEN

The snow was now up to Danny's knees and drifted as high as his chest in spots. Where were all the plows? The snow was coming down too heavily and the wind blowing too roughly for crews to make it out in this mess, Danny reasoned, but he also wondered if he hadn't wandered away from the road. He'd stopped several times behind structures—a huge tree, a farmer's fence—to catch his breath and rest for a moment, but he knew that stopping was dangerous.

He was more than exhausted, and though he'd only been walking an hour, time had no meaning. Only the pursuit of shelter mattered now. He felt no pain, but recognized the danger of that. The cotton gloves and scarf were plastered with icicles, and only the warmth of his own breath gave him any sense of feeling. He wanted to sit down and call it quits—and the pull of that desire was like a siren beckoning to him with irresistible force.

But the sound of Gus' voice within his head managed to drown out the pull. *Don't be a fool. Don't be a fool. Don't sit down.*

And just as the siren's call was beginning to win, Danny heard, *Just a little farther. Look up and over to your left.*

Without really thinking about it, Danny raised his eyes from the snow and looked to his left. He knew with certainty that the house he saw, though larger than any he'd ever picked for refuge, was his salvation. There were no lights on in the house so the residents were probably gone. But even more importantly, he saw an open window. No one who was home would have left a window open. The residents must have forgotten it and left before the weather hit. Danny began to plod towards the gaping hole, not seeing anything now except the dark square within the window frame. But Danny's legs didn't seem to function right. He felt like he was in one of those dreams where his feet were moving and he could see where he was going, but he couldn't seem to get there. The hole didn't seem to grow any bigger.

I don't think I can make it, he silently told Gus. *My legs don't want to move. I can't feel my feet.*

Go to the window.

"I want to sit down, Gus. Let me sit down." His voice was weak against the storm.

You will not live if you don't go to the window.

"It's not getting closer. I'm not getting there."

The window is just ahead. Go to the window.

The argument with his friend had given Danny the distraction he needed to get to the house, and he was surprised when he reached over and felt a window ledge.

The touch of the metal and wood shook him out of his trance, and he gripped the frame with both hands, pulled himself up and over the ledge and into the home, landing in a soft pile of snow. The room itself was almost as cold as the outside, but the howling wind would not cut through his clothes here. Danny raised his weary head and looked around the room. The first thing he saw in the dim moonlight was a lamp tipped over in a corner. Had someone before him already broken in? Then he saw that the bed had been mussed, its covers mostly on the floor in a pile beside the bed. Had the homeowners been forced from their sleep? Would he find their murdered bodies somewhere in the house?

He managed to get to his knees with a great deal of effort, and then using his hands, he pushed himself into a standing position. With some effort, he managed to shut the window.

Heat, he thought. "I must find some heat." He trudged across the piles of snow to the door and tried its knob, but it would not turn. The door was locked. *That's strange*, Danny thought. Why had the residents locked off this room and left the window open. "Damn," he exclaimed as he reached into his backpack. He'd broken into his share of buildings, but he'd never had to break out of a room before. His fingers, which were usually so nimble, didn't seem to want to work; then Danny realized he still wore the cotton gloves. He took them off and reached back into the pack, feeling for the lock pick set he always carried. But even with the gloves off, he dropped the tools several times because his fingers were so cold. Eventually, however, he jiggled the lock and heard a satisfying click.

"Hallelujah, Gus. I'm saved," Danny croaked. His throat hurt from the words.

He was about to swing the door open in triumph when he heard a noise behind him. It was a small whimper that sounded almost like a cat or a small child. Danny turned around and listened, trying to focus on where the sound originated. The whimper was coming from the pile of blankets on the floor. My god, he thought, is someone or something in that pile?

Danny walked back to the blankets and grabbed hold of one end, pulling the whole pile towards him, and then gasped as a small figure tumbled out of the mess.

Who the hell has abandoned this child and left her in this cold, Danny thought. He leaned down and managed to put his hands under the child's arms, then lifted the body up easily.

The person, which Danny saw now was a girl, was so cold to the touch, he wondered for a moment if she was dead, and then remembered the whimper. Without thinking, he scooped up the blankets on the floor and wrapped the small body in them, then carried her out of the room.

The next room was slightly warmer. Danny kicked the door closed behind him and carried his bundle forward into what he guessed was a long hallway, though the light was so dim, he could barely make out the doors that led off into other rooms.

Warm, he thought, I've got to get us both warm. Though it was better than the outside, Danny realized the house's heat must have gone off. He could see his own breath. *But how can we get warm*, he thought. He began moving forward, checking doors as he went.

Danny almost stumbled over a metal structure. Shifting his bundle to one side, he used his other hand to feel what he concluded from spokes and seat was a wheelchair. He set his bundle down on the chair and pushed it forward, stopping at each door and peaking inside, then walking mostly blind to feel around until he determined the rooms were bedrooms. He stopped in one long enough to pick up another bed cover and blankets, which he tucked around his bundle in the chair.

Next Danny came to a bathroom. He felt around the very large double sink vanity and discovered that luck was with him—a candle stood on the edge of the sink, a long lighter next to it.

By the light of the candle, Danny found the shower stall and saw that it was outfitted for someone with a handicap. The light of his candle reflected across a metal seat within the tub that sat on a track leading out of the shower. Danny turned on the shower and was relieved when warm water streamed out. The water had not had time to go completely cold—in fact, it was still mostly hot. He turned back to the bundle on the wheelchair, picked the girl up out of the blankets and set her on the seat in the shower, then found the hand-operated shower spray and let the warm water cascade over her head.

The girl whimpered slightly, showing Danny that she was still alive, though barely conscious.

"What are you doing?" her tiny voice said.

"You need to warm up. I'm getting you warm. Lift your arms up high." He unbuttoned the now soaked gown and drew it up over her head, only to gasp when he realized she was not a child. Although she was small-framed, the roundness and fullness of her breasts and hips told him that she was a woman, not even an adolescent, but a fully grown woman. Swallowing hard, he placed the wet clothes outside the tub enclosure and continued to warm her with the water.

When at last her skin began to feel warm, Danny put the huge towel he found sitting next to the tub around her, then bundled her again in the bedclothes and laid her gently on the chair. He took the candle into the hall and into other rooms until he found one with a closet full of clothes. He picked up a flannel gown, a robe and several pairs of thick socks and found a large sweatshirt he thought might fit him, and then took the clothes back to the bathroom.

Although her eyes were closed, Danny saw from the light of the candle that color had returned to her skin. Unwrapping her from bedclothes and towel, he began to briskly rub her skin with the towel as he dressed her, trying to get her circulation going and feeling himself blush slightly as his ministrations made her nipples go taut. He was glad for the dim light of the bathroom, even though she was still out of it. Danny wondered as he carefully slipped the gown over her head how someone could have skin so velvety. He breathed deeply the scent of her skin, a scent he did not recognize, though it reminded him of the rich earth he remembered from the few times he'd camped in the country. He bundled her in the robe and drew both pair of socks over her feet. Even her feet amazed Danny. They were tiny and looked like a china doll's delicate feet, and Danny realized as he put the socks on that something was disproportionate about her legs. Although she was petite all over, the legs didn't appear to have the muscles they should.

The wheelchair is for this girl.

The girl whimpered, and Danny realized she was coming to.

She opened her eyes slowly and gazed up at him, a dreamy look in her eyes.

"Are you my bodyguard?" she said in a small voice. Then her eyes gently fluttered closed.

Danny didn't stop to wonder what she meant. It was time to take care of himself. He turned from the girl and rummaged through his pack, bringing out the flashlight he knew was there. Holding the light in one hand, Danny rolled the girl and her blankets out of the bathroom and into a large living room, where he saw a fireplace with logs stacked beside it. He picked her up, and then set her on the couch, covering her with the bedclothes as well as a woven afghan that sat on the back of the couch. Then he placed his hand on her forehead and cheeks, wondering if he should wake her fully.

"Are you my bodyguard?" she whispered again. But her eyes didn't even open, so he decided to let her sleep. He built a fire to keep her warm.

By the crackling light of the fire, he stood there just for a moment staring at her face and wondering why this woman, with her delicate features, slightly too long nose, soft skin and long, blond hair—this woman who looked well fed and cared for, and who probably lived in this huge house, had been locked in a room.

But while the fire had warmed his back, his clothes were wet from the accumulated snow and ice, and he knew it was time to bring the warmth inside himself, all the way to his bones. He returned to the bathroom, grabbed his backpack and withdrew a dry set of clothes, set them on the floor beside the heavy sweatshirt and got into the shower to let the warm water do the trick. He remained there for a long time, slowly feeling his blood return to normal and wondering, "Who would leave such a beautiful creature alone in the middle of a storm?"

CHAPTER ELEVEN

Casey awoke with a thought in her head that surprised her: "I'm warm!" She smiled as she pushed herself to an upright position, and then realized she was not in bed about the same time she remembered why it felt so good to be warm—the cold floor, the drifting snow, the feel of someone pushing her off her bed. Someone had left her in a freezing cold room to die!

Then she remembered her strange rescuer, and she looked around the cavernous living room until she spotted him, asleep on two overstuffed chairs pushed together at the other end of the huge fireplace. His feet rested on one chair, while his large frame rested on the bigger chair, curled on his side and facing away from her. A fire crackled in the fireplace, which was the source of the warmth she now felt. He murmured and turned towards her, causing Casey to clutch the warm bedclothes tighter to her bosom, but he was still asleep. One curl, black as midnight, peaked out of the bedclothes he'd pilfered from the guest bedroom.

Is he really the bodyguard Sam sent, come just in time to save me?

The man stirred and turned towards her, his blankets falling away from his face. He was fairly young, she noted, with a rich crop of the black hair and a rugged looking face.

Who on earth would come out in this weather for a job, she thought? Had he showed up in the middle of the night when he wasn't expected until the next day or had she lost track of time completely? Thank God detective Sam Osborne or someone else had thought to get him here in time to save her. But how had he found her in that locked room? Did he bust the door down? Casey didn't think so. In fact, she vaguely remembered being carried, blanket and all into the bathroom, and—*oh god*, was she remembering this right? Had she been naked at one point?

The man yawned then opened his eyes, and Casey was struck by how intensely crisp the blue of those eyes was. The color triggered the memory of him unrolling her from her blanket wrap and setting her gently in the shower. She remembered the look of concern on his face before she passed out in his arms, awakening briefly when she felt the shower, and he cleaned her cuts. She remembered him covering her feet and carrying her into the living room. She remembered how good the fire felt, but then she drew a blank. She must have passed out again.

Such eyes, she thought now as he looked her way, saw she was awake and sat up. Like a sky on a perfect spring day or the waters of her beloved best vacation spot—the Bahamas.

"Hello," he said softly, yawning. "Feeling better?"

"Warmer, that's for sure. How about you?" She stretched, and then drew the covers up as she remembered him putting on the nightgown.

"Good," he answered. "Much better than last night, that's for sure, ma'am. And I appreciate the hospitality," he said, getting up from his homemade bed and walking towards her, a hand extended as if he were seeking a handshake.

"My hospitality? What do you mean, my hospitality? Aren't you the bodyguard I hired? What are you doing in my house!" She drew the afghan even closer to her breast.

"No, ma'am. A passerby. I saw the open window," he replied, but his face reflected disappointment as he took back his untouched hand and turned away and began folding his blankets. Casey decided that he couldn't be that dangerous. If he was going to harm her, he'd had plenty of chances.

"Well, whoever you are and however you did it, I seem to owe you my life. I'm deeply grateful, and I'm glad you're here in the warmth of my house."

He turned back to then, surprise on his face. But his smile was broad and warm.

His folding accomplished, Danny took a long stretch, and Casey couldn't help noticing how big he was with broad shoulders and long legs. He may not be a bodyguard, but he'd make a good one, she thought.

"You hungry? Got anything we can eat?" he asked, and it was her turn to be surprised. But her stomach was empty.

"There's cereal and milk in the kitchen," she said. "But I need to use the bathroom first. Do you suppose you could wheel my chair over here?"

He found the chair, then without asking her, lifted her gently onto the seat, smiling as he asked her, "Paraplegic?"

For the first time since the accident, she felt no embarrassment in explaining why her legs didn't work. Somehow, it seemed inconsequential at this point.

She answered simply, "Spinal injury. Car accident."

"Looks like someone took the battery out of your electric chair," Danny remarked. "I'll look around for it, but let's get you to the bathroom for now."

He wheeled her down the hall and into the bathroom, then left, gently closing the door.

As Casey sat in her chair wondering if she had the strength yet to lift herself off the chair and onto the toilet, the stranger outside knocked softly on the door and asked, "Need some help in there?" Then Casey remembered something else about last night. After he'd warmed her and put on a fresh gown, he'd lifted that gown and placed her gently on the toilet. At the time, she was too exhausted to care.

"Thank you. I'm fine," she said now, determined not to have to go through that embarrassment again.

But she was touched by his willingness to help. This was a complete stranger; she didn't even know who he was. Why was he passing by the house last night in a snow storm? Was he some sort of house intruder—a robber with a heart? But Casey couldn't wrap her brain around that idea. Even though she didn't know him, and he was very masculine and much bigger than her, she felt no danger in his presence.

She heard him leave the hallway after saying, "Call if you need me."

When she was done, she lifted herself back to the chair and rolled towards the kitchen. She heard him coming to meet her at the door.

"I don't know what to call you. What's your name?" she asked.

"I'm Danny Jones. And you are?"

"Casey Lewis," she told him. Then they were quiet as he found the milk and cereal, then an old coffee pot, some filters and coffee, which he put aside on the counter. The light of the window shone through onto his strong hands, and she saw that though his clothes were worn, they were clean. He'd taken off the old sweatshirt of Ricky's he must have found in one of the rooms and left it beside the bedclothes on the makeshift bed. Wasn't he cold? The kitchen wasn't very warm, though she was comfortable enough in thick robe and gown.

But Danny just got to work, looking in cabinets until he located the cereal and pulling milk out of the fridge.

When they'd both had bowls of cereal and milk, he turned to her and broke the silence. "Have you looked outside? It's coming down very hard, though I believe the wind has died down somewhat. I think we're going to be stuck here for quite some time. I hope you don't mind that I took shelter with you. I can help you get through this maybe, if you'll allow me to stay."

She wheeled herself over to the patio door and was surprised to find that snow was half way up the glass door. The blinding white covered everything, but it was breathtaking. "Yes," she gasped, "We may be stuck here quite awhile. But I owe you my life. You're welcome to stay of course." She turned around as she felt him standing close to her and her reaction to his size must have been reflected in her face.

"Sorry, do I scare you?" he asked.

"No," she replied firmly, moving her chair back towards the table. "I may be a fool about many things, but I believe you intend me no harm."

And it was true. She had no idea why, but she felt utterly safe for the first time in a long while.

"Thank you," he said, his voice low and a little in awe. He wasn't used to respect.

Danny went to the stove then and experimented with the knobs. To his delight, he discovered the stove was gas—an older model. Though the electricity was off, they could light the burners with a match. Danny rummaged in the drawers close to the stove and came up with a box of kitchen matches, likely kept there for just that purpose. Though he had originally intended to brew the coffee over the fire, he put the pot on a burner to brew, then opened the refrigerator again.

"I know we just had some cereal, but I'd love something warm and it would feel good in our stomachs. How about some eggs?"

"Yes, we have some eggs, but I don't know how to fix them," Casey confessed, thinking what an odd way of phrasing it—feel good in their stomachs? It would indeed feel good right about now—something to warm them from inside. "Sarah always fixes the food."

He turned around and gazed at her. He didn't know who Sarah was, but he thought it peculiar that this girl didn't know how to scramble an egg.

"Time to learn, I guess," he told her, surprising Casey again. "I'll show you what to do. It's not too hard."

He withdrew the eggs and located a bowl and a fork and set them on the kitchen table. When she made no move to pick them up, he looked at her and said, "Are you telling me you never cracked an egg before?"

Her cheeks flushed. It was true, though. Sarah and Joseph cared for her with great attention and love, but sometimes the attention was a little too intense. They did everything for her—especially the cooking.

What could be so hard about cooking an egg? Why had she allowed herself to become so useless? She had been so full of vigor when she was young. So eager to learn—before the accident. But, she'd also always had servants in the house that did the cooking and cleaning.

Sighing, she reached for the eggs and bowl. "Yes," she said firmly. "But it's never too late to learn. Teach me."

And he did, his muscular hands, twice the size of her own hands, showed her how to whisk the eggs. Then turn on the burner part-way while holding the match to it until it caught, then switch to low heat under a pan. He never left her side and assisted when she couldn't quite reach the stove top.

The eggs truly did taste spectacular. She must have, indeed, been very hungry, she thought.

Danny not only showed her how to prepare the breakfast, he also handed her a towel and asked her to dry the dishes as he washed them at the sink.

It actually felt right somehow, cooking and then cleaning up instead of just waiting for things to get done.

With full cups of steaming coffee, they went back to the living room, and he re-stoked the fire. Casey was just wondering if she dared ask him to show her how to make a fire (Joseph would never allow such a thing, but who knows how long he'd be gone), when she saw Danny look down at his wrinkled khakis. "I think it's time to get dressed. My other clothes should be dry by now. I'll look in the closet and find something warm for you to wear. Do I need to do this for you or can you handle it?"

"I'll be fine," she said, realizing that, while it would take longer, she truly did want to dress herself.

Why do I allow Sarah to treat me like a child, she thought, feeling a tug of impatience at herself.

After struggling into her clothes in the privacy of a chilly guest room, she rolled into the bathroom where she combed her hair and put on a bit of powder and a light layer of lip gloss, telling herself it was to guard against chapping. The makeup somehow made her feel refreshed.

She found Danny, clothed in a pair of heavy jeans and a wrinkled shirt. He was stuffing the khakis into a black bag. She watched silently as he rearranged the contents of the pack to fit. "Do you always carry extra clothing?" she asked.

"Oh, I carry everything in this backpack," he replied. "I call it my 'Gus' pack."

"Everything?" she asked, wondering if he was one of those cross-country hikers trekking across America on a mission.

"Yes, everything I would need in an emergency."

She wondered what type of emergency he might get into, but decided it was probably none of her business. She smiled and asked, "And why is it called a 'Gus' pack? Is Gus a brand name?"

"Hardly," he laughed. "But it would take me some time to explain what I mean."

"Well, we certainly have some time on our hands," Casey replied.

"Okay. I'll start with Gus," he said as lifted her from wheelchair to couch, gave her a warm blanket, then sat down on the floor, his back to the fire, Indian style, wrapped another blanket around his shoulders and leaned back against the chair opposite her.

"Gus," he said slowly, then sighed deeply. Casey could tell Gus was someone important to this strange man.

"If Gus were in this room, you would see an old bum, with scraggly hair and worn clothes. Gus had nothing in this life, but he gave me everything," Danny continued.

Casey didn't know what to say to that. Danny got up and bent over to poke the logs once again. After the logs flared up, he grabbed the chair itself and easily lifted it and placed it closer to the couch, but facing the fire now. He sat in it then, and put his chin on his palms, his eyes turned to the fire.

"Gus rescued me when I was ten and living on the streets. I was starving and frightened—I had been running away from danger for several days."

"From that day on, Gus was with me—not a boss, but definitely my teacher. Not a father, but my fierce protector. He showed me how to survive. God, but I miss him."

Casey looked over at Danny, surprised at the emotion in his voice. She didn't know this man at all, but she reached over and placed her hand on his arm. "I'm sorry," she said. "It's horrible to lose someone you really love. I know—I lost my father and mother when I was thirteen—in a car accident."

He turned towards her then and looked up into her eyes, "I still hear him talking to me, though. Is that possible?"

"I don't know," Casey said honestly, "but what matters is that it keeps him close to you."

Then they were silent, consoling each other

without words or the need to talk. Despite the very different worlds from which they came, they shared a bond at that moment, and that was what counted to both of them.

CHAPTER TWELVE

The town of Lancaster, Pennsylvania was eerily quiet, though that stillness was punctuated by the occasional lonely howl of the wind. The storm had died down somewhat, though the snow continued to fall in heavy layers, and the occasional gusts built piles even higher in some areas.

The entire countryside was covered with glistening white, as if the clouds themselves had fallen from the sky and were resting on the ground. Vehicles that would normally be traveling the roads sat still, covered and waiting for salt and plow trucks to dig them out. The trees were frosted with heavy icing that caused the limbs to reach lower and lower towards the ground.

Lancaster had 60,000 inhabitants and almost all of them sat confined within homes.

In fact, the only activity that could be seen was at the town hall, where thirty snowmobiles were lined up and several four-wheel drive vehicles were parked. The snowmobiles had been volunteered for emergencies as authorities discussed how to handle what had become the biggest blizzard the county had seen in fifty-plus years. Electricity had gone out in all of Lancaster sometime during the night.

But Samuel Osborne was not troubled. He'd awakened cold, then dressed in layers and walked through the small home where he lived, closing off rooms. He now sat at a desk, a gas heater keeping the room warm, the window drapes open for light. He was deeply engrossed in his notes based on files he'd reviewed at the police department. His good friend at the department, Lieutenant Bob McCoy, had come through again and given him a few hours before the storm hit to look over and make copies of the official police reports on the deaths of Richard and Helen Lewis. Over and over, Sam read the notes, trying to make sure he was not missing something. If alcohol was not the deciding factor, as Casey claimed, and the brakes were not faulty, as the police report showed, why had the accident occurred? He also studied his own notes on the attempts on Cassandra Lewis' life, trying to put together the incidents to connect them to a killer. He made a note in his notebook: Who could have been at all these places? Who had the knowledge to rig a platform walkout and didn't have a very good shooting arm? Car color: gray or silver with tinted back window.

Lastly, Sam wrote down: *why?* He studied closely what he'd written about Richard Lewis' two wills. What had made the man suddenly take most of the money away from his business associates and his first family to give to the young girl and her mother?

Sam looked up now and out the window at the falling snow. He truly hoped the young blond beauty so tragically stricken was okay in this storm. He'd called the cell phone number she'd left with him only to get a "circuits busy," then voicemail. He got the same signals, however, from the bodyguard's cell phone, so he hoped that meant the man had ventured out and made it to Casey before the worst of the storm. Certainly a murderer couldn't get out in this weather, so she should be safe at home. Sam peered closer at the files.

CHAPTER THIRTEEN

"I think I should see if I can find something to build a little oven in the fireplace," Danny said to Casey, suddenly taking on a business-like tone after spending the last few hours listening to her read aloud.

After his initial outpouring about Gus, Casey had decided she wouldn't press for more details. She was curious, but she let the silence lie in the air. When at last he'd lifted his head, he'd noted the books on a nearby bookshelf, and they'd gone through them until they located what he said was a favorite of his: Charles Dickens' *Oliver Twist*.

"I know people find the orphan's life grim, but Dickens captures so well the small kindnesses that give the boy hope, as well as the desperation that comes with living on the street," Danny had said.

Casey, who had read the book several times, had quoted a few passages starting with the infamous, "Please, Sir, may I have some more?" then turned to page one and began to read. Danny had simply curled his long legs up in his commandeered arm chair and listened.

Now, Casey watched him get up and stretch, then go into the kitchen. She heard him open the kitchen door and go into the garage. He came back into the living room carrying six bricks and a rack from the oven. At one side of the giant fireplace he placed three bricks, left a space, and placed three more. Then he put the rack on top.

"This will give us a place to keep the coffee heated and cook some food." He moved the logs closer together on the other side of the fireplace, placed a fresh one on top, and then blew into the ashes. Immediately the fire was ablaze again.

"I filled some pans with water in the kitchen, just in case the pipes freeze," he said.

Casey wondered what pans of water had to do with frozen pipes, but decided to let him have these moments to himself. He seemed so in control and focused on his own preparations.

Eventually, he sat down again in his armchair and stared into the fire. "I'm sorry. I didn't mean to clam up about Gus. It's been less than a year that he's been gone."

"I understand. It's been seven years since I lost my parents, but it feels like only yesterday." Her words drew his gaze to her face.

She felt the heat from that gaze, but she said softly, "I'm glad you know so much about surviving in a storm."

"Well, it's easy to survive a storm when you're inside. It's outside that's makes life difficult."

Casey's eyes traveled quickly to his face, wondering if he was feeling sorry for himself, but she saw only a wide grin.

"And now," he said, "tell me about yourself. Start with the accident."

She sighed. "There really isn't much to tell about that. I was thirteen. My mother and father were killed in the accident; I was thrown from the car," she said, a look of pain crossing her face. "The doctors said it shattered part of my spine, and I hurt physically for a long time. But I'm better now. Just don't have the ability to walk. The accident took my legs away from me."

"They look like they're still attached," Danny said, but he was looking at her closely, waiting to make sure she didn't feel like he was poking fun. Casey looked into his kind eyes, smiled, and continued.

"It was late at night and raining. We were just returning from a weekend away—a wonderful party." Her green eyes sparkled at the memory. "My brother and sister were both there and so were most of our family friends. We were a big crew back then and the party was a celebration—a joint happy birthday for Ricky and Ginger, whose birthdays are only a few days apart."

"Ricky and Ginger? Your brother and sister?" he asked.

"Yes, kind of, anyway. Ricky is my half brother, who is seven years older than I am. His mother is Anna Mae, whom our father married before meeting my mother Helen. When my father and Anna Mae divorced, my dad married my mom, who had been married before and had Ginger. So Ginger is my half sister and five years older than me. "

"This is Ricky's sweatshirt?" he asked, pointing to the sports emblem on his chest.

"Yeah," she smiled. "A big Pittsburgh fan. Sometimes, if he's too loaded or he doesn't want to face his mom, he stays here with me. Or at least he used to. He hasn't been here much lately."

"Are you closer, then, to your sister Ginger?" he asked.

"No. Not at all, really. She doesn't come to see me, though she's called a couple of times. I kind of grew up watching her put on makeup and all that idolizing stuff that little girls do when they have older sisters. But mostly she just ignored me or told me to go play.

"The two of them are close, though—Ginger and Ricky that is. Always have been. I guess they just considered me the young brat of the family. I know mom and dad spoiled me a lot."

"Well, I think it would be great to have such a large family. I don't even know who my real parents were. Gus was my family, as well as my traveling companion. But even we had our ups and down and occasionally took a break from each other. What's it like living with someone all time?"

Casey looked at him then, and decided to explain what it was really like with the two of them as siblings.

"The party was special because we were all together and celebrating. It didn't happen often, really. Ginger and Ricky were always getting into trouble and eventually, Ricky went to live with his mom, and Ginger lived with her dad for awhile. It was the first time in a long while all of us were together."

"They weren't happy living with you and your parents?" Danny asked.

"Well-l-l-l—" Casey said, drawing out the word. "They kind of both got booted out because of me," she said. She looked over to see a puzzled expression on Danny's face.

"They were always playing tricks on me, but most of their pranks were pretty harmless. However, they went too far one time," she said.

Danny didn't say anything, just waited for her to continue.

"I was twelve, and it was summer. We had always gone to this cottage on a lake near Alleghany National Forest. Mom and dad told Ginger and Ricky they had to take me for a swim on the lake. It wasn't big, just a small, private lake close to where we stayed. They took a neighbor's boat, a bottle of vodka, probably from mom and dad's supply, and rowed me out to a permanent raft that was rarely used."

But Danny could see that Casey was not upset. In fact, her face took on a dreamy look.

"I was kinda thrilled to tell you the truth. It felt very grown up out there on the raft, Ginger and Ricky giggling and passing a big cup of vodka and Kool-Aid back and forth. They started giving me sips."

"Anyway, eventually the booze must have got to me, and I fell sound asleep. When I woke up, they were gone, it was getting dark, and I was all alone in the middle of a lake. By the time they sobered up enough to realized what they'd done and admitted it to mom and dad, I had been out there for hours. I didn't swim well enough to make it to shore."

"My god, Casey, how cruel! They could have killed you!" Danny exclaimed.

Casey gazed into the fire then and appeared to ponder his words.

"I suppose. Though I wasn't hurt other than a sunburn. Anyway, things were not the same after that, and Ginger and Ricky went to live elsewhere, returning occasionally on the weekends. I guess they always saw me as a third wheel anyway. I know mom and dad lavished attention on me, and I mostly soaked it in, but I also followed my two siblings around like a puppy dog when they were around."

Danny laughed at that, then got up and threw another log on the fire. By now they had been talking for several hours, and the fire had weakened.

"Let's go make a stew for supper," he said suddenly, as if he'd thought of a great adventure. "I noticed meat in the freezer, already cut up. I think it's enough for a stew, and we can find some vegetables and let our stew cook over the fire."

He got her wheelchair and they went together to the kitchen. He opened the refrigerator and pulled out carrots and onions, then pulled the beef he'd spotted out of the freezer and found a bag of potatoes in the pantry. After kneading the beef enough to break the partly thawed lumps apart, he handed her the carrots and a peeler, pronouncing, "You peel the carrots."

"Show me how," she said.

His big hands covered her own as he demonstrated how to peel away from her body into a paper bag he'd set on a nearby chair. Then he set to work peeling potatoes. They were silent as they worked, but the silence was friendly and relaxed. Each was lost in their own thoughts, but they occasionally talked. Danny explained how Gus had taught him to cook during the few months most winters when they'd stayed in a friend's tiny cabin on a lake—their winter haven from the streets, though they'd returned to the city each spring. Danny didn't share with Casey the pain that returning to the city always caused him, but told her how amazed he was when he learned Gus could cook, and how good the meals were after eating fast food during warmer weather.

Casey explained how she was beginning to realize how dependent she'd become on others. Sarah and Joseph had been with the family since she was an infant and had taken over as surrogate mother and father when hers had perished in the accident. But because they'd started as service staff, they still often treated her like a boss and wouldn't have considered teaching her to cook.

Now, here in this kitchen, Danny put the meat into a large, heavy pot on the gas burner. "It needs to brown—makes good gravy that way," he explained to her. He showed her how to clean and chop the onions, laughing when her eyes watered and tears fell on the chopping block on her lap. Danny found some thyme, bay leaves, and garlic powder. He put all of the ingredients into the pot with the meat and added several cups of water. Putting the cover on it, he carried it to the living room, trailed by Casey.

"We'll just let this simmer for a while," he told her, placing the pot on the rack and shoving the glowing embers at the bottom of the burning wood under the oven rack. "Don't let me forget it."

"Is that my job—to remind you?" she said, smiling.

"Indeed it is, as it was always my job as a youngster. We only had the fireplace to cook on in that cabin, but we'd make some marvelous meals—saving our money for a while so we could stock up before we left for the cabin. Those were truly the best of times, and we would have stayed if we'd had any money. Once the warm weather hit, Gus' friend had to rent out the place." Danny had paused as if to keep the memory alive for just a moment. But he quickly got back to the business at hand.

"Now, let's put some more coffee on to brew so we'll have something to keep us warmed up. Then I'll go around the house and make sure the faucets trickle a little," he said, explaining how a trickling faucet kept pipes from freezing. When Casey asked why, he also explained that a frozen pipe could result in no water, which was the reason he'd filled pots.

That night, after they'd eaten the delicious stew that had cooked for hours, along with big chunks of the soft bread Danny found in the pantry, Casey looked for candles while Danny looked for additional blankets. "I think we should be comfortable sleeping here in the living room," he said. "I can keep the fire burning—I wake up every few hours anyway. And I think the wind has slackened a little."

He smoothed out the cushions on the sofa with his big hands, then lifted her out of the chair and placed her gently on top of the cushions, tucking three blankets around her.

He pulled his armchair bed closer to the couch, and then leaned close to her face.

"Thank you for letting me stay here, Casey. I promise I'll take good care of us both and be out of your hair as soon as the storm subsides."

"I'm so glad you found my window, Danny. Stay as long as you need to," Casey whispered back. Then she reached up and touched his face, startling Danny. But he didn't withdraw. She pushed one stray lock of black hair back against his head, then snuggled into the covers and turned away from him. He drew back then and situated himself on the overstuffed chair with a footstool, pulled a couple of blankets over himself and said softly, "Good night."

"Danny," he heard her say, "will you tell me more about your Gus pack tomorrow?"

"I will," he answered softly, just before they both fell asleep.

CHAPTER FOURTEEN

Turning his body slightly, trying to get more comfortable on the overstuffed chair, Danny listened to the wind howl. When they'd gone to sleep last night, he thought the storm was ebbing. Now it sounded as if the giant storm had only paused to catch its breath and was now in the midst of a true tantrum. He pulled the covers closer, trying to get warm.

A small hand reached over and touched his shoulder. "Danny," Casey whispered, "are you awake?"

"Yes."

"The storm seems to be getting worse. I'm a little cold. Is the fire okay?" she asked. In the flicker of the crackling fire, he could see just her face peeking out from beneath a pile of blankets, but he could also see her breath. The heat had been off more than thirty-six hours now.

"The fire is doing what it can," he told her. "It just can't keep up with the air temperature." Danny stood and shook out one of his two thick blankets and tucked it around her.

"No," she protested. "I already have more than my share. I don't want your blankets. You'll freeze."

"I'm not going to freeze. I was just lying here thinking about what we could do to get warmer. Is this the only fireplace in the house?"

Casey reached up and pushed the covers from her face so he could hear her better.

"No," she said. "There are several upstairs in bedrooms and a sitting room. And there's one on this level in the library—but we can't keep two fireplaces going, can we?"

"Where is the library?" he asked her. "I don't remember seeing it down here."

"It's kind of hidden in the middle of the house, really. It was Dad's retreat from Mom, and sometimes the whole world. It doesn't have any windows, and the only access is through the dining room."

"No windows means less cold," he said as he threw his remaining blanket around his shoulders and went through a door to the dining area. A second door off the dining room, a door so inconspicuous he hadn't noticed it, lead to the library. He shined his flashlight around the twelve- by fourteen-foot space amazed at the hundreds of books that lined the walls and the feeling of masculinity the room imparted. Besides the smaller, obviously unused fireplace was a desk and a sitting area for reading with a loveseat and two comfortable chairs with ottomans.

This should do nicely, he thought.

Danny leaned down to check out the fireplace and make sure the flue opened. He returned to the living room and took as many logs as his arms could carry, making several such trips between the two rooms until he had carried all the firewood into the library and stacked it beside the fireplace. He set up some logs, but didn't light a fire until he'd returned to the garage and kitchen for bricks and another oven rack, which he used to build a smaller cooking area on one side of the fireplace. Finally he lit the fire, and when he could feel its warmth on his hands, face, and chest, he knew the room was ready. He returned to that room and scooped Casey up, blankets and all. They dragged on the floor and at one point; he set her down on a chair to pull most of the blankets off, wrapping just one thick one around her small body.

"Don't want to trip and drop you," he whispered in her ear as he picked her back up.

She snuggled closer to the warmth of his body. "Why are we moving?" she asked, her voice soft and drowsy.

"The living room was just too big," he told her, "And there were too many windows fighting against the wind." Danny set her down in the love seat and left to recover the rest of the blankets and the water pan in the fireplace. He put the blankets on the wheelchair and held the pot of water in his other hand to wheel back to the haven of the library. He set the pan on the new fireplace oven, then returned to the loveseat and, pausing for a moment, seemed to make a decision. He picked up Casey again, and holding her gently, turned and sat down on the loveseat, tucking many covers around them both. At first, Casey was stiff in his arms, unaccustomed as she was to being held like this. But she understood the necessity of keeping their bodies close and once they were situated on the love seat, she let her muscles relax and laid her head against his chest.

"Sleep now," he whispered. "I'll keep you warm."

She snuggled deeper into his chest and without thinking, put one arm around his waist before returning to sleep.

When Casey awoke the next morning, alone but warm, she could hear the faint sound of singing. With sleep still weighing down her mind, the sound startled her. Was the radio playing? But as she woke, she remembered the events of the last day and recognized that the voice was Danny's. He had a low, but melodic singing voice, hitting most of the notes right on target and sounding joyful and light, though Casey couldn't make out the words. Struggling to sit up, Casey tilted her head as if the motion could bring the song closer. When the library door opened, it was as if the sun had magically appeared in the small room. Danny stood in the doorway, a tray with two steaming cups on it, and a wide smile on his face.

My, but he's a handsome man, she thought as her eyes traveled from the deep black hair to the rugged, but pleasing features of his face and his smile, and then downward in a long sweep that took in how long his torso was.

"You have a beautiful voice," she said, and saw his face turn just a tinge red.

He'd added another sweatshirt to what he wore, and it made his upper body seem even more massive than before. She'd felt the strength in those arms last night as he kept her warm and protected. She shook off the last remnants of sleep as she reached to accept a cup of hot chocolate.

"Good morning," he said. "Did you finally get warm last night?"

"I certainly did. It was the nicest sleep I've had in a long time."

His blush deepened, and he looked away from her face.

"Everything is white outside," he mumbled, trying for a more comfortable subject. "Even the sky is white. In fact, you can't see anything but white out there."

"Maybe we're in heaven," she said softly, but then realizing she was just embarrassing him, she added, "What have you been up to this morning?"

"I've been exploring the house. We're definitely in the best room to stay warm, but I found some interesting things. You must have gone camping a bit because I found some gear in your attic," he told her.

"We camped only a couple of times. Dad liked it a lot—Mom wasn't too crazy about it. She preferred the comfort of a Marriott."

"Well, I found two sleeping bags that will help us stay comfortable," His voice made his discovery sound like presents on Christmas morning.

"And best of all, two marshmallow forks. We can use them for toast this morning. Drink your hot chocolate, then we'll get washed up and ready to cook."

Casey really didn't know how she was expected to make toast with a long metal fork, but she laughed at his enthusiasm. After she had taken care of the bathroom, given her face a quick, now freezing once-over with a washcloth, and struggled into another layer of clothes Danny had brought her, she wheeled back into the library to find Danny with bread and jam from the kitchen. He showed her how to spear the pieces of bread and how close to the fire to put the stick. The toast took awhile, but somehow this morning the charred piece of bread that resulted, with a thick layer of jam, tasted as good as a croissant at a French café to Casey.

When they were done and had discarded the breakfast dishes in the kitchen sink, deciding to wait for warmer water to attempt to clean them, they returned to the comfort of the library. They stuck their feet in the sleeping bags and laid back in the love seat side by side.

"Tell me more about Gus," Casey said, hoping Danny was ready to talk. "He seemed like someone smart enough to hold down a job if he'd wanted to. Why was he homeless?"

"He never talked about how he came to the streets," Danny said. "Not even once. When I asked, he just repeated, 'the past is better left there.'"

"You never found out anything?" Casey said, turning to study his face. A small smile appeared there, along with a gleam in his eye.

"Gus didn't know this, but I got some information from a nun he once left me with while he went to find work. I was only small when he left me there in her care for a couple of days, but when I was older, I found the church where she'd been. Even though I was young when he left me, I sensed that the two of them knew each other well.

"Sister Rose said Gus actually had graduated from a pretty prestigious law school and had been a lawyer, when his world fell apart. He had a wife and two children, but like many young lawyers, he was a workaholic. One night, when he was supposed to be home for a special occasion of some type, the whole family was murdered by an intruder. Gus was the prime suspect, but not for long. He had dozens of witnesses there at work with him and eventually, evidence showed it was a random burglary. The murderer was caught and jailed, but for Gus that mattered little. He hadn't protected his family—hadn't even thought about them that night before the police showed up at his workplace.

"He spent the next two years in a mental institute and couldn't work at all when he got out. He spent quite a few years drinking away his sorrow, but that had stopped by the time he found me."

Several tears found their way down Casey's cheek, but Danny would not let her cry.

"Casey, it was a very long time ago and neither you nor I were there. We're here now, safe and warm and part of the reason is Gus and what he did for me. Now let's change the subject. What were you like as a girl?"

Her tears turned to laughter then. "I used to be a real bitch."

Surprise lit Danny's eyes. "Geez, A brat and now a *bitch*. I have trouble imaging you that way!" he exclaimed.

"You have to remember, Danny, that I was Mother and Dad's love child. I was cute and blond and the exact opposite of my two trouble-making half-siblings. We were rich, and I was a very spoiled child. I could do no wrong in my parents' eyes."

"That couldn't have made your brother and sister too happy."

"Oh, I gave them lots of reasons to resent me—at least I recognize that now. I certainly didn't when I was young, and I don't think Mother or Dad really intended to be so prejudiced. It's just that both had horrible marriages before. Ricky and Ginger were the results of those marriages while I was a result of falling in love. Ricky probably never had much of a chance with Dad, but for two years, before I came along, Ginger had been the little darling in their lives. That stopped with my birth so it's hardly any wonder she never liked me."

Danny turned to look at the blond-haired, green-eyed beauty that sat next to him. *How could anyone dislike this woman?*

"So you were a little spoiled! That doesn't make you a bitch."

"Oh, I practiced that in other areas. I was raised to treat the Lindquists as servants, and I took full advantage of that. I would boss them around and then blame them for anything and everything that went wrong. I think I even blamed them for the accident, right after it happened. Well maybe not blamed exactly, but they were there as I went through physical therapy. They were there as I withdrew from the circle of friends that were no longer friends because the chair frightened them. And as I learned to deal with my parents' death at the same time I was dealing with being confined to this wheelchair, I fought them every way possible. Oh, I was truly horrible to them for a long time. I don't know why they put up with it, I really don't."

"You were just a kid—and you were hurt and angry," Danny offered.

"They gave me nothing but love and care during those first three years. In return, I battled with them all the time, refusing to acknowledge my disability or their efforts."

Danny got up then to stoke the fire and think for a moment.

He turned towards her when he returned to the loveseat and reached out to stroke the light golden locks.

"I guess we both had it pretty rough growing up, but I guess we both had some help."

She took the hand that touched her face and placed it in her lap.

"Yes, Danny. If the Lindquists taught me one thing, it's that love can creep in despite your best efforts to keep it out. I treated them like enemies, but their patience and diligence won out in the end. I began to see them differently, though it was a gradual process.

"And now, I couldn't live without their love, as well as their care."

CHAPTER FIFTEEN

S am was truly worried now. It had been three days since the storm hit and the land-line phones were still out. He didn't know if Michael Moorhead, the man he had set up to get to Casey's side as soon as possible, had succeeded. He couldn't imagine Michael letting his cell phone die so soon—the guy was a real techno-geek. Surely he had backup batteries.

Unfortunately, Sam himself hadn't been so wise. He hadn't had a land-line set up in his house yet, just his office—who needed one with cell phones today? Sam liked his privacy when he wasn't working.

He'd spent much of yesterday calling around using his cell, checking on people he knew in the area, conducting a little business until the land-lines in town went down completely. He hadn't really had more than a few fleeting thoughts about Casey and the fact she might be alone. About seven that night, he noticed his battery was getting low. He'd made a final call to Michael, and then shut off the phone to conserve the battery. He turned it back on this morning, hoping for a message. He tried once more to get in touch with Michael or Casey, and then spent the last of the juice calling local authorities to alert them to Casey's situation. But while they'd listened patiently, a single individual caught in a blizzard was not a priority in an emergency like this no matter whether she was confined to a wheelchair. Police could barely keep up with the calls coming in. A very polite woman took down the information about where Casey lived and promised they'd have someone check on her as soon as an officer with a snowmobile was available.

Sam tried to bury himself in a crime novel, but his mind kept returning to the young girl whose hand had trembled when she'd asked for his help. He finally put the book aside and got out his notes from his interview with her lawyer. He studied the will of Richard Lewis and couldn't help wondering what had happened to make the man change the original provisions.

He finally got up, went into the kitchen and made himself a sandwich. When he was once again back in his chair, covered with blankets, his dog Buddy curled on his lap, his thoughts wandered into the past, a place he usually tried to avoid. With nothing else to occupy his mind, however, the past invaded his quiet.

Marrying Barbara had been a mistake, and he felt no longing when he remembered the decade they had together. They had very little in common—she was a night person who loved the social life and spent many evenings drinking with friends and dancing. He had little desire to go with her and spent most evenings at home. The only good thing to have come from their union was Davie.

Sam frowned and picked up his book. But after trying to read a few sentences, he put it back down and pulled the covers up to his chin.

Davie had tied Barbara and Sam together for a short while. The boy had been a constant joy for both of them from the day he was born. He brought laughter and love to a home that had mostly lacked both. God, how Sam missed that feeling and the boy who had created a family— if only for a short while.

Without realizing what he was doing, Sam began to stroke Buddy's soft fur, waking the snoozing dog.

It had been a little over seven years now, and despite years of searching, Sam had no idea whether his son was alive or dead. His young son had been snatched right out of a sporting goods store as Sam stood in line to pay for the badminton set Davie had picked out as a birthday gift.

Barbara had blamed Sam, but not nearly as much as Sam had blamed himself. The marriage had collapsed under a giant bubble of grief, anger and frustration and so had Sam's job on the police force as a detective. He had left the force when his captain had demanded he let the kidnapping case drop—Sam spent too much of his time and all of his effort searching for his son. When the time came to decide between keeping his job and dropping the search, he'd quit and started his own business as a private detective. The first two years, the business barely scraped by. After two years, however, Sam's own father had died, leaving Sam a hefty sum of money that had changed everything. Now Sam only took cases that interested him, cases like the attempts on the life of a young girl confined to a wheelchair and about to inherit a fortune. Sam threw back the covers and took up his notes again. But he felt frustrated and helpless. If only he knew she was safe.

CHAPTER SIXTEEN

Sam would not have been worried if he could have seen the house on the edge of Lancaster. At the moment when Sam had been using the last of his cell phone juice to talk to police, Casey was curled up in blankets, sipping a cup of hot coffee. The six-foot-four-inch, solidly built Danny was beside her, sipping his own coffee. What Sam couldn't have known was that Danny would have done battle with anyone who harmed the petite beauty who sat next to him.

At the moment, they were silent, staring at the fire, but comfortable in the silence. They had already shared a lot about themselves with each other, more than either of them had talked about to another single individual over such a short amount of time.

Next to the fireplace was Danny's worn backpack. Casey's eyes fell on the pack, and then turned to Danny's face.

Such full lips—how could they look so pillow soft after being exposed to this fierce weather.

"Tell me about your Gus pack?" she said.

Danny's eyes left his coffee cup and traveled to her face, which at the moment was framed with blond hair sticking out every which way from the blanket that encircled her. But his eyes found hers and stuck, drawn into the green lightness of them. He smiled, and rose from the loveseat.

"Sure, Casey." He walked over to where he had put the pack and brought it back, placing it on the floor beside them.

"Gus called this pack my lifeline—and it has proven to be true many times over. I've carried it with me every day since Gus stocked it for me. He put essentials in it he said would get me through most days."

Casey didn't have anything to say to that. She had no idea what it was like to carry your possessions on your back. She threw back the covers, though and bent over to try and lift the pack, feeling how heavy it was. There must be many items inside.

"Where did you get the money to buy the things in there?" Casey asked.

Danny turned to face her.

"I've added a few things over the years, as odd jobs and money has permitted, but I've often wondered how he afforded that first batch. All I know is that he put together the pack after an ugly incident."

"An incident?" Casey asked.

Danny put the pack on his lap, but didn't move to open it. He sat back on the seat and gazed at it, remembering a day long ago.

"Gus left me all alone one day, as he often did while he went off to stand at the gas station where men came by to find extra day workers. He'd usually be back in several hours because there wasn't really much work to be found.

"Anyway," Danny continued, "that particular day, Gus told me to stay where he had settled me. I usually did; but for whatever reason, I was restless. I climbed out of the big box I was sleeping in because I heard some young boys in the alley. I just wanted to play with them, but they had no desire to 'play' at all. They began to tease me, pinching and slugging my arm. It made me angry, and I was foolish enough to kick one of them good in the shins."

His eyes returned to the fire

"After they beat me up, I managed to crawl back into our box to hide. When Gus got home later that day, he was very angry because I had a huge black eye and cuts and bruises all over my body. Gus did not anger easily."

Casey covered one of Danny's hands with her own, wishing she could have given the small boy the same comfort.

"He knew he couldn't pursue whoever did this to me even though I was scraped raw. And I was going to be OK. But the next day, he took me to a large house beside a very large church. Remember Sister Rose I told you about?"

Casey nodded her head.

"The first time I saw her, she scared me to death! Here was this rather stout woman surrounded by black robes with just a white cap and collar sticking out. I guess I hadn't seen many nuns," Danny said with a laugh. Then he took on an Irish accent.

"'Ah, Gus, what d'ya have there?' this vision of black and white said to us, pointing at me and my bruises. She didn't seem to be accusing him of anything, just curious about me. I shrank behind Gus, tears in my eyes, certain he was going to leave me with her just as every social worker had left me with strangers in the past. Gus, however, pulled me around gently in front of him."

"'This is Danny,' Gus said, 'and I need a safe place for him to stay for a few days, Sister. You've offered to help me so many times, and now I'm asking you for that help. I'll be back Friday for him. You have my word.'"

"Sister Rose didn't even question him further. She just smiled and said something like, 'we'll take good care of him, Gus.'"

"Gus then leaned over and said in my ear, 'I mean it, boy. Four days.'"

Casey studied Danny's profile then, envisioning the frightened young boy who had found a hero and had to go through the fear of losing him.

"I don't know why this woman never called social services. I guess she'd seen enough kids go through the system, and she must have trusted Gus. At the time, I was absolutely sure I was going to be put in jail or sent to a new foster home. But the Sister kept me warm and fed."

Danny looked at Casey then and saw that she was still focused on his words. Her mind had traveled with him back in time envisioning his past.

"I never found out exactly where Gus went, but probably to a rougher area of the city where he didn't want me to go. But true to his word, he returned in exactly four days.

"'Tomorrow, son,'" he told me, 'We buy everything for your lifeline pack. I won't be around forever to take care of you. And it's time you took care of yourself.'"

Danny opened the backpack and began to take out items to show her. First came a pair of rubber boots, which he held up for her to see. "I thought when I saw my first pair of these that they were foolish and stupid looking. And they added a lot of weight to the pack, even when I was young and had a smaller size."

He paused then, and looked deep into her eyes.

"But these probably saved my life two days ago," he went on.

He then began pulling other items from the bag and explaining their use, sounding almost like a teacher lecturing his students.

"To survive the elements, you need both a heavy coat or hunting shirt and a waterproof jacket. That's because some days it's just cool, sometimes just cold. But in cold weather with precipitation, like snow, you have to be able to stay both dry and warm. Thermal underwear and layers are essential."

Then Danny pulled out a long woolen scarf. "This will protect your ears and neck, but it also has other uses. I've used it as a rope, protection for my hand when I had to break glass to get in a building, once I even used my scarf for a tourniquet when a friend was knifed and losing blood."

Casey shuddered then, picturing Danny trying to save a friend bleeding from a knife. She wanted to know what happened, but didn't want to interrupt Danny's presentation.

"You also need multiple pairs of socks—both for warmth and to use for mittens, if you don't have gloves at the moment," he added.

"And I've always carried two complete sets of clothing," Danny said, pulling out a pair of khaki pants and a wool shirt, "as well as a better pair of shoes than the ones we wore most days."

"Why do you need good shoes?" Casey wondered.

"Gus taught me that when you live on the street, there are places you can go as long as you aren't taken for a street person, which is why you always have a set of clean clothes and better shoes," Danny explained. "When the weather was really foul, we spent nights at shelters and occasionally days. But, when the weather was okay, we were on the street, sometimes seeking work and quite often at the library," he said.

Casey was puzzled, "The library?" she asked.

Danny sat back on the loveseat, his arms relaxed at his side, the backpack temporarily forgotten—his face reflecting the pleasure of a good memory.

"The library is one of the greatest places to hang out, whether you have a home at the moment or not. It's warm in winter, cool in summer; it has quite comfortable chairs where many people—homeless or not, doze off for short periods of time."

"But best of all, the library has books," Danny said with wonder. "Hundreds and hundreds of books on any subject you can imagine, and you don't have to pay for *any* of what you read. Way back when Gus and I first hooked up, he had a driver's license probably from his earlier years. He got us both cards, which the system just kept renewing," he said.

"Those books were my schooling, my entertainment, and my babysitter on a lot of days when Gus had to go off to work," he continued.

Danny sat forward then and returned the items to the pack, zipping up its main compartment.

"I talk too much," he said, momentarily embarrassed. "This is really boring."

"Oh, no, please go on," she begged, and Danny realized that his life was so different from hers, no matter what he said, it was new and fresh to her.

"Okay, Casey. If you're sure." Then he unzipped another compartment and pulled out a plastic zip bag, opened it and slowly laid out the contents, "A toothbrush and a container of baking soda. The baking soda works like toothpaste—but it also serves as a salve for bee stings and insect bites. And if you have no soap to wash your clothes or you have to wear them more than a couple days, you sprinkle soda on them, and it removes some of the odor."

Casey was astonished at what she was hearing, but she didn't doubt that he'd used the items he carried frequently.

Danny then laid out a small box. "Aspirins for headaches or body aches, vapor rub and cough drops for colds and most important, antibiotic cream for cuts." He chuckled lightly at Casey's amazed face.

"And just those medicines and those few items kept you alive all these years!" she exclaimed.

"That and the guidance Gus gave me. Oh, and a couple of trips to the emergency room," he answered, but then he continued talking without explaining those trips. He stopped pulling out the items he was referencing, though.

"You also need a small candle and matches for steady light in places that aren't hooked up to electricity. We usually had a flashlight for dark nights when we weren't sure what noise we were hearing but wanted to find out fast. I always have a cup to collect water and occasionally use as a dish. And a comb and razor to clean up. That's about all—except for a billfold with at least $1.25. When it got down to the $1.25, we knew it was time to find more work," Danny said.

"$1.25?" she questioned.

"Yea, you'd be surprised what you can buy with a buck—a small hamburger, a bowl of chili, French fries—all of those will keep you from going hungry. And you need the twenty-five cents to make sure you have tax."

After considering whether he should show her a final object, he dug deep into the bag and pulled out a complicated looking tool.

"And you can't live without a Swiss army knife, the kind that has several blades and scissors, a screw driver, and some picks," Danny said. He looked at Casey and decided to tell the truth.

"One of these picks can open most house locks and another can get a car door open."

He saw the look of concern on her face, but added quickly, "We never robbed anyone, but sometimes we did find ourselves needing to climb into an abandoned car for its warmth, or inside a deserted home or building."

Casey's face relaxed, then, as she said, "Gus gave a great deal of thought what to put in the backpack."

"Gus gave a great deal of thought to everything he did," Danny said. He looked into the fire, before turning back to her and smiling.

"And that concludes the secrets of my Gus bag."

"Gus must have really been extraordinary," she said.

"Yes," Danny replied. "He really was."

After several hours of reading *Oliver Twist*, Casey suddenly put the book down and turned to Danny.

"Since I'm now a gourmet cook, how about I take lead chef position tonight, and you can be my assistant," she said. "But first we need some firewood. We're about to run out."

Danny chuckled softly, and then got busy with the task she'd assigned him. They both bundled up and met in the kitchen.

Casey smiled as he came into the room and nodded her head at the potatoes.

"Your turn to peel."

As they sat at the kitchen table, Danny turned to Casey. "I have to ask you something that really bothers me." He stopped peeling. "How did you end up locked in a room in the dead of night with an open window?"

A shadow crossed her face as she gently laid the bowl she was using on the table.

"Remember when I asked you if you were my bodyguard that first night?" she said. "Didn't you think that was a strange thing to ask?"

Danny looked at her closely then. "At the time, I was barely thinking, just reacting. Later, when we were warm, I guess I assumed you felt I saved your life so you were calling me your bodyguard."

"Which you did, of course," she said. But the shadow remained on her face. "There's a lot more to it than that, however. I was expecting a man from town to show up that I've hired as a bodyguard."

Danny's eyes widened and he sat back in his chair.

"A bodyguard? Why do you need a bodyguard? Who do you need protecting from?"

"From the person who has been trying to kill me."

Danny's brow wrinkled in concern.

"I remember being angry when I first saw you," he said, "thinking you were an abandoned child. But by the time I realized you weren't a child, my mind was on getting us warm."

"Well," she said, a note of anger creeping into her tone. "I was pushed out of that bed by someone who opened that window, then locked the door from the other side. I guess whoever it was saw I was unconscious, then dragged my chair out of the room and pushed my bed-pull away so I couldn't reach it. He took my cell phone, and then left me there to freeze!"

"My God, Casey. Who would do that to you? And why didn't he just kill you then?"

"I don't know. I suspect it was supposed to be some kind of accident that happened to the poor handicapped woman alone in the house."

She resumed beating the eggs in the bowl, a little too roughly this time.

"I've hired a detective and I have some ideas. But whoever is trying to get to me has tried four ways now to get me out of the picture, and he seems to be getting closer to succeeding," Casey said. Her movements were stiff, her face set in a frown.

"Why would anyone want you dead?" Danny questioned.

"My theory is that it has something to do with me turning twenty-one. My birthday is only weeks away."

"What does that have to do with anything?" Casey looked up from her bowl.

"I inherit all of dad's stock in the company as well as the bulk of his estate." Casey sighed deeply. Danny just looked confused.

"My half sister, half brother, Dad's two business partners and his business manager were given some money in the original will Dad wrote. But something made him change his mind. He changed his will and basically cut them out. He set up trust funds for Ricky's mom, my sister and Ricky, but they end when I'm twenty-one."

"Do you know what happened to change his mind?" Danny asked. He resumed peeling, and Casey resumed her tale.

"Not for sure. Maybe it had to do with the raft incident I told you about. I know Dad was furious after it happened, but it was a couple years before he changed the will. Daddy already didn't get along with Anna Mae—they fought all the time. Anna Mae runs the company now, but at the time she was in charge of sales and spent most of her time out of the office—otherwise I don't think they could have stood being around each other. I guess he just got disgusted at the lot of them."

"But why did he cut out the business partner and his own manager? And why would any of them harm you?"

Casey's eyes filled with tears.

"I have no idea. All he really did was not give them a lump sum. John still works for the company, and Reggie is a minor business partner. It wasn't like he gave either of them much in the first place."

Soft tears were now running down her face, but Danny didn't think she'd even noticed she was crying. She probably spent many restless nights thinking about all of this—he decided to let the subject drop for now.

The two continued working on eggs and potatoes, then took their finished dinner back to the living room, bundled up in the blankets, and ate side by side in silence.

Suddenly Casey's head turned towards Danny, and her eyes traveled over the bulky blankets that surrounded his larger form.

"So," she said, "I need a bodyguard. Would you take the position?"

"What. *Me*?" he said, his eyes round. "You'd hire me? But you already hired someone!"

"So what. I don't want a guy I don't even know. I want someone I can trust—I trust *you*. You've taken great care of us during this storm. I see no reason that can't continue!" she said.

"Thank you for that. I'll think about it," he whispered. He got up and poked the fire before returning to the loveseat. Without really thinking about it, he bent over and planted a tiny peck on her cheek. But Casey reached up and framed his face with both of her hands. She made Danny look into her eye, and then she pulled his face down towards her and kissed him fully on the lips.

"Thank *you*," she whispered, when she was done.

He stared into the green of her eyes, still tasting the honey of her lips and wondering what she was thinking and why she had done that. And wanting to give her back the enthusiasm he felt in the kiss, but knowing it wasn't a good idea.

CHAPTER SEVENTEEN

Casey and Danny spent a restless night. After Casey pulled Danny to her for the kiss, they parted awkwardly to separate sleeping places in the now comfortable library. Danny dragged couch pillows in from the living room and warmed them by the fire, then crawled on top in a sleeping bag. Casey settled back against the love seat, curled up under many blankets and feeling warm throughout for the first time in several days.

But neither could fall asleep. As they prepared for bed, they hadn't said more than half a dozen words—the easy conversation and companionship of their two days together replaced by unease.

Casey's mind turned to the year before the accident. She was twelve—a golden year of awakening to her own femininity—the year she began wearing panty hose, had gotten her period, had a different boyfriend every few weeks. She hadn't thought about those times in many years—too embroiled in bitterness, and then gradual reawakening that required putting the past completely behind her. The years right after the accident she'd tried to return to her old school (after a year in hospitals and recovery centers) to find out that, not only had she lost her support system—her mom and dad—but her world was forever changed. Boys were polite, but distant. Most girls avoided her almost entirely. Teachers were overly helpful. She'd kept herself busy with extra schoolwork and just rolled through each day helped along physically by Joseph and Sarah and feeling comfortable only in the cocoon of her familiar house. She'd graduated high school a year ahead of time and attended a two-year business college she could take mostly online. Once she'd gotten an associate's degree, she'd used her trust fund to travel with her caretakers to exotic places that could accommodate a wheelchair. Only recently had she begun to ache for more, though she had not yet defined what that was.

She dated a bit during her last years of high school and for a few years afterward—mostly blind dates set up by friends or family. But the men she'd met, while a few had been nice enough, didn't seem to really see her, just the chair.

Casey turned to look at the soft rise and fall of the sleeping bag. She pictured his big hands on hers, showing her how to peel potatoes. She saw in her mind the easy smile that came in the middle of a discussion. Despite the awkwardness of the last hour before bed, their conversation had been more comfortable than any she'd had with anyone in as long a time as she could remember. His knowledge base appeared to be as wide as hers and wider in certain subjects. They discussed historical events and debated their significance. They'd analyzed what their favorite authors were really trying to say. But what she didn't understand was why she felt so comfortable, but yet so feminine. Somehow his strength and size didn't make her feel like a helpless girl caught in a wheelchair—it made her feel like a woman.

Casey sighed and turned back towards the couch cushions.

The rise and fall of the sleeping bag stopped as Danny turned to lie on his back, his eyes still closed. He was not asleep, just trying hard to calm himself. Unlike Casey, Danny didn't have much experience with dating. He'd spent his teen years simply surviving. Then, the years before Gus died, Danny and Gus' roles had switched. Gus had become frail and Danny had learned how to care for someone—both physically and mentally. He'd kept his caregiver fed and warm and spent most of the hours when he wasn't looking for work talking to Gus about the things he'd learned.

This woman on the couch awoke a tingling he could compare only to the excitement he felt in learning something or seeing something new or amazing. But the tingle felt uncomfortable at times. He was pretty sure she had no idea how his body reacted when she stretched and yawned, her blond hair curling every which way, messy and unrestrained by hair bands or styling. His thighs and hips and what was in between tightened now as he remembered looking over and suddenly falling deep into the green of her eyes, then withdrawing and wondering what she might look like beneath the multiple layers of clothes they wore.

Who am I kidding, Danny said to himself, feeling slightly nauseous. He turned back to face the fire, not even wanting to look in her direction. He had no formal education, hadn't been inside a classroom since the third grade.

He couldn't even get a full-time job without a social security card or permanent address. He didn't think a library card from Washington, D.C. was going to help him much should he ever find a place to settle.

Danny had seen in her face and felt in the warmth of her hands that that her kiss was not innocent. He had no idea how many men she'd been with, but he didn't want to be one of them. Despite her offer of a job, he knew that once the storm was over, he'd be on his way to the city, and he didn't want to leave her with regrets about their time together

Danny opened his eyes and stared into the roaring fire, wishing it could burn away his restlessness.

CHAPTER EIGHTEEN

On the fourth morning after the storm hit, the town of Lancaster was finally calm. The fierce winds had stopped, and although snow was still falling, it was a gentle covering on top of piles that were deep enough to cover some of the residents' cars.

Only a few houses had electricity, and all the shops were closed. The only signs of life outside were children building snowmen or tossing snowballs at one another. It was great fun for the little ones, who knew they'd have no school for days. But for many of the big ones trapped inside, trying to cope with no lights, no stoves, no television and no computers, the feeling was more of disaster than festival. After several days, they were tired of eating sandwiches, drinking cold tea and playing cards. They were even tired of making conversation with their own families and the occasional neighbor.

Many residents were simply bored and ready for their world to return to normal. When the first snowplow showed its face in the late afternoon, those who saw it felt a sense of hope. It's not that people wanted to be at work, quarreling with co-workers and looking forward to the weekend. It was just that many of them had forgotten how to live life without power and convenience.

Inside the house at the edge of town, two young people were still sleeping.

Suddenly someone was banging on the door, loudly calling out Casey's name. "Casey. Casey Lewis, are you in there?"

Go away, Casey thought. *I don't want any visitors.*

But her eyes flew open.

Visitors—in this storm?

"Danny. Danny, wake up. I hear something."

Danny was on his feet in seconds. He grabbed a poker and spun to face Casey. But then he stopped and cocked his head.

"Casey Lewis. Casey, this is the police. We're going to break down the door."

A look of panic crossed Danny's face.

"Danny," Casey said. "I'm sure it's okay. Go get the door before they break it down."

But Danny stood motionless.

"Then bring me my chair, Danny. I'll answer the door!"

Danny came to his senses. What did he have to fear from local police?

When Danny opened the door, he saw only one uniformed cop standing on the stoop, looking half frozen. A snowmobile was parked on the front lawn and a path of deep footprints lead up to where the officer stood.

"Oh good," the cop said with a laugh. "I don't think I could have budged this door. I would have had to break the glass!"

But then the cop stiffened as he took in the large man still holding a poker aloft.

"Lancaster PD," the police officer said. "And you would be?"

"Danny Jones, sir." Danny put the poker down to his side. "What seems to be the problem?"

"I'm looking for Casey Lewis, who lives here. Detective Sam Osborne said she was left alone in the house."

Danny said the first thing he could think of. "She's fine, Sir. I'm her bodyguard. Please come in." He held wide the door and let the officer pass.

When the policeman got to the fire, he held his gloved hands out in gratitude. But he got down to business quickly, turning to Casey, who Danny had just introduced.

"Sam Osborne called us, Ms. Lewis. He was concerned that you had been left all alone. He explained that he'd hired someone, but wasn't able to get in touch with him."

"It was extremely thoughtful of him to check up on me. Officer Pendross is it?" Casey said.

"Yes, ma'am. And this man with you is the bodyguard, you say?" Officer Pendross said, peering closely at Casey as if trying to weigh whether she was telling the truth or under pressure to lie about who Danny was.

Casey glanced at Danny and back at the officer. Should she tell the police the truth at this point? But in the middle of this snowstorm, she couldn't see what that would accomplish. She quickly composed her face as she replied, "Yes. Bodyguard and chauffeur. I've hired him to look after me, and as you can see, he's done an excellent job," she said, smiling and sweeping one hand around the room. This did not seem the time to try to explain who Danny really was and that someone had tried to harm her. And she was pretty sure the policeman would assume Danny was involved. There would be time after the storm to sort out what was happening.

"Yes, you seem to be quite comfortable here," said the policeman, looking around the cozy room and spotting the logs by the fire, the grate to one side, the multiple blankets and sleeping bags, and the pot that held yesterday's coffee.

Seeing him looking towards the coffee pot, Casey said, "Can we offer you some hot coffee? It was wonderful of you to check up on me—we could get some brewing pretty quickly."

"No, give me a few more moments of this warm fire, and I'll be on my way. We're actually starting to dig out this morning, but there's much to be done. I'm checking on a few people we're concerned about." The officer looked at both Danny and Casey and grinned as he added, "Mostly what we're finding is that the people of Lancaster hunkered down like you; they've handled the storm just fine. The power may even be on sometime tonight or tomorrow."

Casey smiled warmly in return. Danny bowed his head and chuckled softly, imagining the police force expecting disaster among the houses they visited, but finding people warm and safe in their homes.

Casey saw Officer Pendross glance over at Danny.

"I'm just glad people are okay," she quickly added. "And we really appreciate your concern."

The policeman's eyes were drawn back to

the blond girl.

"Well, I've got a pretty long day ahead of me. Better be on my way."

Danny showed the policeman to the door.

A pot of coffee, another breakfast of slightly burned toast, and a half hour of silence later, Casey's soft voice interrupted Danny's thoughts.

"You never answered me really, Danny, when I asked before. I need someone I trust at my side—someone to protect me and maybe drive me around. Will you do it?"

Danny looked over at the young girl almost swallowed up by the blankets around her. She looked so fragile.

Casey was holding her mug just in front of her mouth, the steam rising slowly.

"I'm not a real bodyguard, Casey. I don't even have a high-school diploma. And what was that about me being a chauffeur?"

She chuckled softly.

"I didn't really think about it. You said bodyguard. I said chauffeur. It seemed to make sense."

Danny saw, then, the determination in her eyes as she looked at him.

"You don't have a job at the moment. You're a good caregiver. You could help Joseph and

Sarah. It won't take you long to get a driver's license."

Danny shook his head slowly as if trying to take in the information she was throwing out. Then he ran a hand through his hair. "What about the guy you already hired?" Danny looked around the room, and his face hardened. "Besides, I hardly think I fit into this world of yours." But when his eyes returned to her face, he was surprised again—this time at the spark of what looked like anger.

"And what world is that, Danny? I don't know anyone who is living a life like mine. I am mostly alone, except for Joseph and Sarah. I'm not working, either, though I intend to do that one day. I don't have any idea what I should be doing with my life, though I've at least come out of the feeling-sorry-for-myself shell. But I know one thing: I won't get anywhere until someone catches this guy who is after me. I am sick and tired of being scared—and one thing that these past few days have given me is some peace."

Casey paused before adding, "I can pay you to keep me safe; you need the money. You could use the stability of having an address to get a social security card and a driver's license. Why wouldn't you want the job?" But she wasn't looking at Danny. Her eyes were focused on the folded hands in her lap.

Danny rose then from the love seat and knelt in front of her, taking one of those hands in his.

"Why in the world would you hire some guy who shows up in the middle of a snowstorm—a guy who has admitted he's homeless?" He saw her eyes soften then, and she put one palm against his cheek.

"You make me feel safe, Danny. I don't know why, but that's the bottom line for me. I really do need your help. And I'd rather have you as my guard than some stranger I don't know."

Then she covered his big hand with her small one.

"I know it's a sudden thing, Danny. But don't you want a job?"

"And where would I live?" Danny looked around the room again, but this time, he wasn't looking for the contrast between her life and his. He was just taking his environment in. And when his eyes returned to hers, Casey could see he was at least considering the possibilities. She threw back her covers, pulled her chair close and plopped into it.

Taking his hand, she used her other hand to maneuver towards the garage. Once they were there, she pointed to a door at the other end of the cavernous, but empty room.

"Open that door and go up those stairs. Dad created quarters for household help years ago—for Joseph before he married Sarah. Now Joseph and Sarah have my entire second floor here in the big house. Just go up and see for yourself."

Danny crossed the garage, opened the door, climbed the small staircase and paused at the landing. Looking around, he saw a two-room apartment. He could see into both rooms from his vantage point. One held a bed and an old-fashioned television; the other had a couch, chair and kitchenette.

"Would something like that do?" Casey yelled as she rolled to the bottom of the stairs.

He came back down the tiny staircase and took her hand again. "It's a great little place, Casey."

"Well, it's yours if you'll help me," Casey said.

A smile lit Danny's face as he began to believe it could work. "You mean this, don't you?" he said. He knew the arrangement might not be permanent, but it would give him more time to get to know her, to not have to worry about his next meal, to allow him to explore the possibilities of what he could do with his life.

When they were settled again in the comfort of the library, back to being side by side on the love seat, the mood of uneasiness that had afflicted them earlier was completely gone.

"Why in the world can't our lives have crossed paths for a reason?" Casey said, looking over at him. "I'm tired of being scared, and I know I don't know you well, but I believe in you, Danny. You can stay here rent free; I can pay you a small salary. Part of what I can offer is to use my computer. You said you learned about the Internet at the library. There are all sorts of online possibilities now for bettering yourself. It helped me get a degree."

In answer, Danny just took her hand in his and pulled it close to his side.

CHAPTER NINETEEN

Late in the afternoon of the fifth day after the storm began, Detective Sam Osborne came knocking at Casey's door. The police department had assured him that Casey was okay and that there was someone there looking out for her. However, the man Sam had hired had finally gotten through to Sam's recharged cell phone earlier that day to explain he'd been delayed first by a run-down car and then by the storm. The cop who had checked on Danny and Casey had not raised any alarms, and Sam was sure the bodyguard was either a relative or someone Casey had hired at the last minute, but he needed to make certain. The main roads were mostly cleared, and Sam's four-wheel drive would get him up the lane to her house. Casey's phone service had not yet been restored, and she wasn't answering her cell.

The guy who answered his knocks certainly looked capable of keeping her safe. He was at least six foot three with broad shoulders, not stocky or overly built, but with a strong handshake and relaxed smile. Sam immediately felt better.

But within fifteen minutes of conversation, he was no longer quite so comfortable. Casey explained about the opened window, her brush with freezing to death, and Danny's rescue. What were the odds that this guy came along right in the nick of time?

It would do no good, however, to alienate him right away, Sam thought.

"I'm sorry the guy I tried to hire didn't show. How lucky that you were passing by and saw the open window. You're obviously very good at this guarding stuff. Where did you train?"

Danny narrowed his eyes as he looked over at Sam. But he sat back on the couch and sighed.

"I hope to learn on the job, Sir. I am not trained in law enforcement. Casey was just lucky I was hitching and saw the open window. Before I came through that window, I was stranded in this storm with everything in town shut down. I thought I was a goner until I saw that open window. I honestly thought no one was home. So you see, I was lucky, too." Danny looked over at Casey, his eyes lighting up.

Sam studied the young man's face as Danny talked. After years as a detective, he was fairly confident in his own judgment, and he honestly felt the fellow was telling the truth. Besides, if he had a criminal background, Sam would soon know.

Danny and Casey were a half hour into filling Sam in on Danny's background, when a second knock came at the door.

Ricky and his mother Anna Mae peeled off their cashmere scarves and leather gloves as they came into the library.

"Quite a storm out there, huh, Sis," Ricky said as he looked around the room. Unlike the big living room, he wasn't familiar with the library. But he located the decanter nevertheless and poured himself a glass of refreshment.

Anna Mae's eyes went immediately to the two men in the room.

"And you would be?" she asked, one eyebrow cocked upwards.

Sam reached forth and offered his hand.

"Sam Osborne, ma'am. And this is Danny Jones," he said, offering no further explanation.

Anna Mae turned her head then and focused on Casey.

"Visitors? In a storm like this?" she said.

Casey sighed. Did she really need to explain herself?

"Not exactly, Anna Mae. Sam is a private detective I've hired to look into the attempts on my life, and Danny is my new—Danny is looking after me while Joseph and Sarah are gone."

"I see." Anna Mae's eyes traveled the length of Danny from his worn boots to his slightly grungy jeans to his wool shirt, lingering briefly on his face. She did not, however, look displeased at what she saw. Her eyes had lingered on the broad shoulders and sturdy arms. She turned back to Casey.

"Well, my dear. I supposed if it helps you feel better to have a, man, around the house. But really. A detective?"

"Would you like a cup of coffee, Anna Mae?" Casey said, motioning towards the pot resting on the coffee table. Casey did not go so far as to lean over and pour into one of the spare cups on the tray.

Anna Mae waved a hand in dismissal.

"I'm afraid we don't have but a moment. We're on our way into town to stock up. But as you can imagine, we were terribly concerned for your welfare in this vicious storm. I'm greatly relieved to see that you have someone here with you. You know how much I worry about you. I'm glad to see your power is back."

But Casey could see Anna Mae checking out Sam then, her eyes glancing sideways at him. Apparently, she decided to pursue her curiosity no further at the moment, though, because she looked back at Casey and said, "We'll be on our way then. I just need to use your ladies room. Ricky, gather our things, and I'll be right back."

Ricky's face showed his disappointment as he gulped the last of his drink, and then put his glass on the table. As Anna Mae headed down the hall, he picked up his scarf and wrapped it around his neck. Then he picked up both pairs of gloves. A few minutes later, when Anna Mae returned, he handed her a red pair.

"Well, Sis. Glad you're okay. Mr. Osborne. Mr. Jones. We'll see ourselves out."

When they were gone, Danny and Casey resumed filling Sam in and brought him up to date on what had happened.

"I was sound asleep but something woke me up," Casey explained. "I felt for the lamp by my bed—it wasn't there—nor was my cell phone on the stand. I pulled myself up to a sitting position and tried to look around the room, but my eyes weren't adjusted, I guess. I certainly don't remember seeing anyone. But I do remember being shoved off the bed. I must have hit my head and blacked out."

Casey looked at Danny, then, who continued the story, "When I found her, she was rolled up in her blankets like a sausage in a bun. I almost didn't see her at all. I tried to leave the room, but the door was locked from the other side."

Casey picked up the tale, "When I woke up on the floor, I tried to crawl to the door, thinking I could get out and find help. I'm afraid I sat there and bawled like a baby for awhile when I discovered it was locked. I didn't know what I was going to do, which is why I pulled down the covers and rolled into them. I was so cold." Despite the now-warm room, she shivered.

"I knew I was going to die. I *would* have," her eyes softened as she looked at Danny, "if he hadn't saved me."

Sam was silent for a long moment before he spoke, "And you did not get a sense of this person? Male, female? "

Casey shook her head and answered simply, "It happened too fast, Sam. It was too dark. I didn't have time to think before I hit the floor. But whoever it was, was strong."

Sam took a sip of his coffee, then opened his notebook and looked at his notes.

"I've been reviewing what little I know so far—the attempts on your life as well as your parents' deaths. I wanted to ask you, Casey. Why were you so certain your father wasn't drunk at the time of the accident?"

Casey's looked a little embarrassed then, but raised her head high as she recalled how she felt, "I was thirteen, and I thought I knew it all back then. Two weeks before the party, I caught my father in a drunken stupor—I was appalled, and I let him know it. The next day I begged, pleaded, and threatened my dad that I'd tell my mom if he ever was drunk again. The night of the party, I watched him like a hawk. I told the bartender that he was not to serve my father more than one weak drink. I even went around sniffing any liquid he had beside him. I behaved rudely, and I'm sure my dad knew what I was up to. But I know for a fact my father had maybe one drink that night. I don't know how strong the one drink was, but he switched to club soda towards the end of the evening. I was shocked when the police said alcohol probably played a role in the crash."

"I told the cops my concerns when I was able to do so. But I'm afraid it was several weeks after the accident before I could be interviewed in any depth and by then, they'd already concluded the accident was caused by his blood alcohol level. The autopsy showed he had a slight blood-alcohol-level, but it was below the legal limit.

The phone rang and Casey cocked her head.

"Oh, good. The phones are back on. Let me just see who that is," she said, wheeling over to the phone.

Danny and Sam sat in silence as Casey talked on the phone.

"Of course, I'm okay, John. Why wouldn't I be okay? Yes, they left as planned, but I had a person here looking after me. Who?"

She looked over at Danny and grinned.

"Oh, I've hired someone to stay with me here in the house and to drive me around. Yes. Yes, of course we can talk about the audit when things calm down. Thanks for calling, John."

She hung up the phone and returned to Sam and Danny.

"That must be the hundredth time that man has inquired about the audit," she said.

Sam looked up. "The one that's to be done on your twenty-first birthday?" he asked.

"Yes. I haven't scheduled it yet, and both he and Uncle Reggie keep bugging me about it."

"Any particular reason they might be nervous about it?" Sam asked, looking closely at Casey to determine her reaction.

"Oh, well. John's the business manager and a stickler for details. And I guess Reggie is just concerned with the business since he's a minor partner."

Sam drew a question mark on his notebook.

"And Anna Mae? Is she asking about this audit also? She is the top executive of the company, right? You think she'd be anxious that everything checks out."

"Anna Mae, from what I hear, is a fairly hands-off manager. She's very good at what she does, which is to negotiate contracts with new pharmacies and distributors. She can really turn on the charm when she's trying to sell. It's what got her into the company in the first place—my dad hired her as a sales manager. But she leaves the business operations up to Reggie and John. Reggie for the administrative and day-to-day stuff and John for all the financial dealings. When the major decisions need to be made, they bring Anna Mae into the picture."

Sam studied Casey's face as she gave out this piece of information. Casey had been looking at the fire and talking freely when she mentioned John and Reggie. But when she spoke of Anna Mae, her eyes drew back to rest on her hands in her lap. Her posture stiffened.

"And how were your father and Anna Mae able to work together after being married and divorced?"

Casey looked up from her lap into Sam's eyes then.

"I think Dad was her first hard sell. He didn't talk about her, but I asked once why he married her. He admitted she completely captivated him at first, though being the consummate professional, they worked together for a year before he finally asked her out. They dated only a few months before they married—they had Ricky within the year. Although their marriage lasted only a few years, Ricky seemed to be a common link. I guess they worked things out for his sake."

CHAPTER TWENTY

And now, Casey, I have to ask you again. Who do you think stands to benefit from your death?" Sam asked.

Casey shook her head, but Sam saw sadness creep into her expression. The three of them had been talking for an hour now—coffee now cold. They'd only been interrupted one more time—a call from Uncle Reggie, checking up on her.

Although heat had returned to the house, Danny got up and went over to poke at the fire.

When it was once again crackling cheerfully, Casey finally answered.

"I know I'm not really close with my family, but I just hate to think it might be one of them."

Danny turned from the fire, still holding the poker, turning it over in his hand as if to inspect it from all angles.

"Has your family and your father's business partners always been so attentive, visiting and calling all the time like they did just before the storm and today?" he asked.

"No," she admitted. "They visited a few times in the hospital but pretty much ignored me after the accident. Well, Ginger still does ignore me. We haven't been close in a long time. But that first few months, only Uncle Reggie came to see me. I don't know why, but in the last year, they've been checking up on me a lot. I know the trust funds get cut off after my birthday. Maybe they all think I'll see that they're taken care of. But no one has come out and asked anything of me."

Sam turned a page in his notebook and looked up. "Your father's will gives you his business on your twenty-first birthday," Sam began. "After that you can do whatever you want, run it, sell it, give it away. Do you think getting that company might be something someone else doesn't want?"

"As far as I know, the company is doing well under the thumb of John and the remaining partners, Anna Mae and Reggie," Casey said. Her forehead wrinkled as she added, "Up to now, I haven't really taken an interest in the company. I haven't needed to—it's sort of run itself."

Sam looked closely at Casey's face to gauge her reaction to what he said next. "If there's any funny business going on with that company, it gives anyone who might be involved very good motive for getting you out of the way."

But Casey shook her head.

"I just can't see it. I'm not exactly close to John Hutchins, but he has been my daddy's business manager for many years. I can't see daddy as fool enough to work with a dishonest person. And Uncle Reggie—" she turned to gaze out the window as if she could see past the distance to his home.

"He's a partner, as is Anna Mae. But our families also used to be close. I called him Uncle for a reason. I know I haven't seen much of him in recent years—he's spent a lot of time trying to get Ellie comfortable. But a motive? Both Reggie and Anna Mae will do well if the company does well. So I can't see anyone trying to kill me because of the company."

Sam sat back in the chair he occupied, letting his hands rest on the chair's arms.

"Money is one of the top motivators in the murder business," Sam said, his voice even, but firm. "And as far as family, you have to realize

Ricky Lewis and Ginger Johnson are your only living relatives. Your dad didn't write into his will what happens if you're not around. He surely could not have foreseen both he and Helen dying at the same time.

"But if you're out of the way," Sam continued, "I'm pretty sure the courts would give whatever money is left over in the estate to your next of kin."

Danny shook his head, then came to sit beside Casey as he added, "Guess it's less complicated to be without all this money." His attempt at humor had no affect on Casey, however.

Sam leaned over and patted Casey's forearm, then got up to put on his overcoat. Casey and Danny accompanied him to the door.

"In any case, Casey, you need to be on guard around those people—all of them," Sam said. Then he looked at Danny. Danny and Sam shook hands.

"Keep her safe," Sam said as he left the house.

Casey and Danny were silent as they returned to the living room. When they were once again seated before the fire, Casey turned to her new friend and protector.

"They wouldn't harm me," Casey said. But her words felt hollow even to her.

"I won't let them," Danny replied

Joseph and Sarah returned the next day. Sarah's sister Lucy had come through the operation with flying colors, and Casey's caregivers had been frantic to see for themselves that Casey was safe.

They fussed and fretted over the house; cleaning Casey's room, which was now wet and dirty from melted snow; restocking the refrigerator, where many things had spoiled; opening drapes that Danny had drawn to keep warmth in the house.

They accepted Casey's explanation that Danny was the bodyguard she'd hired, and insisted on cleaning the apartment in the garage before they allowed him to move in.

Casey and Danny had packed one of the old suitcases in the attic with the few leftover clothes from Ricky that fit the bigger Danny so he'd have something to "unpack" when he moved in.

Danny moved his backpack and the suitcase into the apartment and now lay on top of the covers, gazing at the ceiling, thanking God for the warmth of his new home, and Casey's friendship. He contemplated his future through different eyes than those that guided him forward to this house during the raging storm.

A picture of Casey in her chair appeared in his mind. Her long light hair, green eyes shaded by light long eyelashes, and skin that always looked slightly pink, silky smooth and as unblemished as the snow that now blanketed the town. What would it be like to run both his hands over her face and down her neck—to tangle his fingers in the abundance of gold that framed her face? Several times, as they sat side by side on the loveseat, he had envisioned picking her up and settling her on his lap as he had once they moved to the library, but pursuing the passion he felt when she had grabbed his face and kissed him.

Danny was glad Joseph and Sarah had returned. He loved being in Casey's home. But they both needed the time and space having the couple in the home could provide. He needed to find a comfortable spot in her life—a place where he fit—or he needed to be on his way.

Thank you Gus, for getting me here. But now what?

Two hours later, he emerged from his new home and came to the living room to find his vision staring into the embers of a fire.

"Are you all right?" she asked, the green of her eyes now focused on him. "Joseph and

Sarah retired for the evening, but I was worried about you."

He plopped his large frame into the same chair he'd slept in that first night.

"I fell asleep thinking about this whole situation. I'm not used to options," he said.

"I've been thinking, too," she said, turning her chair toward Danny and rolling closer. "You're very smart, Danny. You're well read and Gus did a darn good job of teaching you how to think. I don't think it would take you long to get your GED, then you could get some training or go to college—"

Danny's head snapped in her direction, but his expression immediately softened, and a smile emerged. "How do you know how smart I am?"

"All you have to do is open your mouth and out comes the smart." She leaned over then and gently slugged him in the arm.

Danny rubbed the spot she'd hit, but his mind was far away. He turned then to look at her, his face settling into seriousness.

"And then what, Casey? I'm glad I'm here. I'm glad you hired me. But I intend to earn my keep and be on my way."

"Oh," Casey said. Then she turned her chair back away from him to gaze again into the fire.

They sat in silence for several minutes; Casey turned again towards Danny, raising her head to look straight at him. "You have the rest of your life to find your way, as do I, Danny. But in the meantime, I need you to help me figure out who's trying to kill me."

CHAPTER TWENTY-ONE

Sam rubbed his hand over his face and yawned. He'd been glued to his desk for several hours, researching what he could about Casey's case by phone and computer.

He looked down at his notes on Joseph and Sarah Lindquist. Joseph was almost sixty five and had been with Richard Lewis for about twenty-five years, serving his early years as the butler. Joseph's wife, Sarah, was ten years younger than her husband. She'd been a household manager for Helen's family for two decades, and then went with Helen to Richard's home after her divorce and remarriage. Two years after Richard and Helen had married, Joseph and Sarah also wed. After Richard Lewis' death, the couple had stayed on to care for Casey, and according to Casey, were her lifeblood in the dark days that followed her parents' tragic deaths. Sam had confirmed by phone that morning that the couple had indeed been visiting Sarah's sister the last few days.

Sam stretched and looked at his watch. He had arranged for the couple to meet him here in his office so that he could talk to them away from the house.

Ten minutes later and right on schedule, a knock sounded, and Sam let them in. Joseph declined coffee, but Sarah asked for a glass of water. The couple sat side by side on the office couch, holding hands and looking slightly uncomfortable at being interviewed.

"Tell me what you saw when you found Casey dangling from the tree roots," Sam asked.

At Sam's words, Sarah turned her head away, a look of pain on her face. Joseph squeezed her hand.

"I don't know that I've ever been so frightened in my life," he said. "Well, up until the shooting incident that is. But we really thought this was just an accident. Casey had been gone about two hours, which was at least an hour longer than she'd been out before on that path. Sarah insisted I go looking for her despite Casey's repeated requests to be left alone on these walks."

Sarah looked at her husband, and the muscles in her face relaxed.

"And thank God you did, Joseph," she said.

"I saw almost immediately as I walked up that something had happened to the walkout. It's on the steepest portion of the path, but clearly visible from the main walkway. What should have been there—railings, the decking—it was all gone. I thought for sure at first glance that she had gone right over the edge."

"Until he saw her hair," Sarah interjected.

"Until I saw her hair. I ran towards that blond, realizing that she must be clinging to something if her head was visible. But that's all I could see, Sam, her head. No chair, no structure, just a head of hair. She was faced away from me, clinging desperately to the roots of the tree, the remaining pylon. I got closer and realized she was hanging by her own strength and her scarf. I managed to grab hold of the scarf and Casey and pull.

"But I tell you, Sam, that once she was safe, I looked back at the walk out, and the whole platform was gone, except for the one foundation post. Her chair lay at the bottom of the ravine, along with all the boarding. Casey says it didn't go down all at once, but sort of collapsed in the middle, then eventually fell apart and fell down the hill."

Sam flipped back through his notes and said, "The contractor, William Clark Landscaping, says there was nothing unusual about that particular structure. It was built the same as the rest with that main support beam and good sturdy wood that should have lasted years. I'm taking him out to look at the remains as soon as the snow clears so we can get to it, though I'm not sure what we'll find after six months. But let's go on to the shooting since it's the only reported incident."

Joseph reddened slightly then, and Sam saw the couple exchange a look. Joseph's eyes returned to Sam's face—the embarrassment gone.

"I did report the car incident, and even the platform collapse, just not at the time they happened. We didn't really start to put it all together until the third attempt, the shooting. When we met with police after that happened, it all came out in the interview—the collapsed structure, the careening car. It had only been two weeks since that car nearly ran down Casey, and we were still reeling from that."

Sarah's voice cut in, then, laced with what sounded to Sam like anger.

"I know we must have sounded nuts to them. We were putting it together as we went. They didn't seem to take us seriously, and we certainly had no proof to give them. All we really had was a bullet in a tree."

Sam looked up from his notes.

"I'm sure they are looking into it. It happened only a week before the snow hit so it's not like they've had a lot of time to investigate."

"You're probably right," Joseph said. But he didn't look convinced. "Anyway, when the police questioned me, I couldn't give them any ideas about who the person was. I saw nothing. The police went over the place they think the shooter stood with a fine-tooth comb but found nothing they could link to a murder attempt. I could give them no license plate for the car, just a vague description—a silver or gray SUV. I picked out three different models it could have been when the police questioned me. And as far as the platform, well—it had been six months," Joseph continued.

The room was quiet except for the scribble of Sam's pen. The detective sat back in his chair, pulling the notepad onto his lap and looking at Sarah, then Joseph.

"We'll go together to the police to report this latest attempt, though with all this snow, I'm not sure we'll find much. We'd be in a better position, here, if you hadn't cleaned up the room."

"I didn't think. I couldn't think—I was so frightened for Casey. The room was just a mess, and I clean up messes—" The pain had returned to Sarah's face. Joseph covered her hand with his.

"We are not detectives, Mr. Osborne. We didn't think in terms of evidence, just Casey's safety and comfort. Snow was piled inside the window, and the floor was soaked, the broken lamp in a corner, her book and her glasses and the water glass lying on the floor."

"I understand, Joseph. We'll still have the room dusted for prints, and we may get lucky and find something, though I'm sure in this weather the person had on gloves. Tell me, then, in your cleaning efforts, you never found Casey's cell phone or part of her phone?"

The Lindquists exchanged another look, and then said in unison, "No."

Sam's second visit that day was to Reginald Stone, who answered the door himself, pulling Sam in quickly and motioning for him to wait in the living room. Reggie then hurried up the stairs in response to a female voice calling his name. Sam couldn't make out what the woman said, only a shrill demand.

"I'm sorry," Stone apologized as he came back down the stairs and into the living room, "Ellie needed me. What can I do for you, Detective Osborne?" He motioned then towards a couch and chair and the two men sat. Sam withdrew his notebook.

"I'm investigating some of the incidents that have occurred to Casey Lewis," Sam said, deciding to withhold mentioning the latest attempt. "I understand you drive a Lexus?" Sam said.

Reggie stood up suddenly. "Where are my manners, Mr. Osborne? Would you like something to drink? I can make us a pot of coffee."

Sam peered up at the other man's face then, but noted only fatigue.

"You have heard about the attempts against Casey's life?"

Reggie sat back down.

"I've talked to her about this—at least briefly. To tell you the truth, Mr. Osborne, I didn't really take her seriously. Frankly, I was quite surprised when you called. And to answer your question, yes, I own a Lexus. It's the one luxury I've spent money on since Ellie's illness."

"Do you own any other vehicles?"

"Well, we have another vehicle that is outfitted to cart Ellie, my wife back and forth to the clinics and the hospital. It's a gray Ford Explorer XLT. But, why are you asking me this?" Then realization seemed to creep in. "You think I had something to do with what happened to Ellie with that car?"

Sam didn't answer his question. "Where were you on Wednesday, January 13, late in the afternoon, Mr. Stone?

"Off the top of my head, I have no idea. Probably here, or the office, or maybe the hospital. I don't really go anywhere else. Why? Why are you asking me these questions?"

Sam ignored him again. "Do you keep a daily calendar of your activities perchance?"

"I have a Blackberry, Mr. Osborne." Reggie stood again and went to a desk.

When he returned, he flipped through the screens of his device. His voice, however, had lost its friendly tone.

"I have no appointment marked on that date."

Sam looked up from his notebook, saw how stiff Reggie's posture had become and sighed.

"Mr. Stone. At this point, I am simply looking into what happened to the people in Casey's life on the dates of the incidents. I want to cross as many people as I can off the list of who might be responsible. I'm not singling you out. Just gathering facts. Do you have anything marked on January 27 at two p.m.?"

"You're acting like I need an alibi. Are those the dates of Casey's 'accidents'?"

"Casey is convinced they were not accidents, and there has been an additional incident. We are looking into all the possibilities. I just need you to verify your whereabouts if you can?"

Just then, however, Sam heard another shrill demand.

"I'm cold, Reggie. Can you bring up the wool afghan? *Reggie!*"

Looking embarrassed, Reggie rose and grabbed the thick blanket on the end of the couch. He took the steps two at a time, the blanket in his hand. Sam took the time to study his environs.

The furniture was sturdy and ornate, expensive-looking, but worn in places. A few oil paintings graced the walls. A fine layer of dust covered most surfaces, though in general, the room was neat. Sam wondered why, with the salary Reggie was making, the couple didn't have a housekeeper. Had the medical bills become too much to handle?

When Reggie came back down the stairs, he was still holding his Blackberry.

"On January 27, two p.m., I was at the doctor's office, Mr. Osborne. You can verify that with his office. On January 13th, I was at home with Ellie, but in the early afternoon, she had a coughing attack. I was concerned enough to call the doctor and meet him at the hospital. She spent the rest of that night and the next morning at the hospital, and I was with her."

"Reggie, who's there? Who's visiting? Can you bring me my book on the living room couch?"

Sam wrote down the name of the doctor and the hospital, but realized he wasn't getting anywhere. He'd get Reggie's thoughts down later—call him into the office or the police could question him. Now, Sam stood and reached to shake Reggie's hand, but Reggie had already turned his back in dismissal and was climbing the stairs again, this time with a book tucked under one arm.

CHAPTER TWENTY-TWO

Sam stood outside a massive oak door and reached for the ornate knocker. He could have simply used the doorbell, but the knocker, with its brass lion's head, fascinated him. He couldn't resist the urge to pick it up and see if it was as heavy as it looked.

A few moments later, a tall, thin woman with Hispanic features wearing a neatly aproned uniform answered the door, a scowl on her face.

"Si, yes?"

"Is Mr. Hutchins at home?"

Without another word, the woman ushered Sam in the door and closed it behind him. She said nothing else, but began walking.

Sam followed her to a richly furnished office. A large desk chair and two high-backed wing chairs in front of the mahogany desk were covered in deep red leather so dark it almost appeared black. The shelves were lined with leather-bound books, neatly aligned. A giant thin computer monitor sat on the corner of the desk, but Sam saw no keyboard. Behind the desk was a gray and brown oil painting of a hunting scene—a single man holding a shotgun pointed across the marsh, hound dogs poised in the distance, a duck falling from the sky.

When John Hutchins appeared several minutes later, however, Sam tried to imagine this guy hunting in a marsh. Hutchins was immaculately dressed in an expensive charcoal suit with a tie that matched the silk handkerchief peeking from one pocket. Every hair on his handsome head was in place.

Sam's host extended a hand, but Sam noted how clammy the handshake was and how stiff the giver. It felt more like a formal gesture than a greeting.

"How can I help you, Mr. Osborne? You said this was in reference to Casey Lewis?" Hutchins didn't move towards his desk or the overstuffed couch in the room, but stood instead just inside the office door. Sam decided to get right to the purpose of his visit. He'd already explained that he was looking into the attempts on Casey's life.

"I understand you own a 38-caliber Smith & Wesson revolver. May I see it?" Sam asked.

John's face lost its formalness for an instant. Sam could see he'd surprised him with the bluntness of the request. But surprise was quickly replaced by annoyance.

"I know that Casey has some weird idea that someone is trying to kill her, but I find it insulting that you would consider me a suspect. I am her father's business manager, and I've looked after Casey's financial interests in this company for quite some time now."

The expression on Sam's face did not change. He was used to the I'm-so-insulted comment as an opening line.

"I'm just reviewing the facts of this case, and someone shot at Casey with a 38-caliber pistol. The police have verified who might be involved in her life that had such a gun, and your name is one of several. I'm just trying to eliminate you by comparing the gun to the bullet. We can't get an exact match, but we could eliminate your weapon."

John fiddled with the knot in his necktie. "Do you have a warrant? If you want to see something of mine, a personal possession, then I require a legal request."

"No. I have not yet obtained a warrant. I was hoping for cooperation," Sam said. He opened his notebook, despite the fact John hadn't invited him to sit.

"I'll cooperate once you have a warrant," John said in dismissal. "Is that all?"

It was Sam's turn to be surprised. He'd been blunt by asking first to see the gun, but he hadn't expected such a cold reception.

"No, it's not all," Sam said. He flipped open his notebook and looked at the first page.

"Can you verify your whereabouts on Wednesday, September 16, of last year and on January 13th at four in the afternoon?"

"That was six months ago and more than three weeks back! How am I supposed to remember back that far? What are you accusing me of?" John narrowed his eyes. "This is all very insulting. The police questioned me briefly after the shooting a couple weeks ago. If you want any information other than what's in their report, contact my attorney, Frederick Miller. I am on my way out the door to get to the office."

John gestured towards the doorway. But Sam did not move. The two men stood awkwardly inside the office.

"I am not accusing you of anything. Just following up on what's been investigated. The police asked for your gun, but didn't have time to collect it before the storm hit. I understand you were out of town when the shooting occurred, anyway. I just want to note where you were the other two times someone tried to hurt Casey," Sam said. "And I wanted to ask you about how the company is doing. Since you're the financial guru, you know better than anyone else."

John's face clouded then, and he shut his eyes momentarily. Sam wondered how much of a temper the man had beneath his Brooks Brothers exterior. John's eyes opened, and Sam glimpsed that anger softly boiling.

"I don't feel I need to justify my whereabouts. I don't believe for a second anyone tried to murder Casey Lewis. I was questioned by the police after she reported the shooting. They did not ask me about those other two dates, one of which was more than six months ago. I have nothing further to add."

"So be it. I'll leave the questioning up to the police," Sam said, shutting his notebook and turning.

Once outside, Sam took a gulp of fresh air. He couldn't quite figure out this man. He knew from his research the guy had an advanced degree in accounting. Casey's father had trusted the man, and the business had done very well in Richard's absence. So why was he so defensive?

Sam headed for his office. He had already spoken to Lieutenant McCoy about search warrants for the gun he knew John Hutchins had, as well as a similar model registered to Ricky Lewis, Casey's half brother. He'd stopped by the Hutchins place before the warrants could be served because it was on his way to the office. He'd wanted to see how the man would react, but he hadn't expected such resistance.

A call to Hutchins's lawyer and then to Bob McCoy affirmed that after the police had talked to John about the shooting, the law firm had backed up his claim that he had been at an out-of-town convention on the day of the shooting by submitting testimony from five people at the convention. The testimony had been submitted into the police report, and while the reporting officer had noted John had no such alibi for the afternoon the car came close to hitting Casey, the investigation had gone no further before the storm hit.

I'll say this for the man, he's got a good lawyer, Sam thought.

Sam drove to the courthouse and talked to the officer that would be serving both warrants. He had been granted permission to be present at the searches.

In the meantime, he'd drop in at the Lewis residence. Sam used his cell to call the Lewis home and let them know he was coming.

The door to the Lewis home had no brass lion, but was as impressive as John Hutchins's entrance. It was also made of oak, but instead of solid wood, the top half had a round beveled glass panel, intricately patterned with occasional spashes of color. A bright red rose stood at the center of the panel.

Sam used the doorbell. Anna Mae Lewis answered the door. She was dressed for the office in a turquoise suit that looked like it was tailored for her shapely figure, tapered at the waist and cut low at the lapels. A hint of lace covered any flesh the suit coat did not cover.

She ran one hand over her jet black hair, which was pulled back into a bun at the nape of her neck, but extended the other towards Sam, who had stepped just inside the door.

"Mr. Osborne. You're a bit late. I'm afraid I only have a few minutes before an appointment at my office. I have a busy day, I'm afraid. What did you want to see me about? You said this has to do with Casey?"

Sam entered the foyer, stamping snow from his boots onto a heavy welcome mat. But Anna

Mae was already turning to pull a heavy wool coat off the coat rack.

Sam decided to see how this cool woman would react with the same approach he'd taken with John Hutchins.

"I understand your son Ricky Lewis has a 38-caliber gun. I'm wondering if I could take a look at that gun, please."

Anna Mae turned to face him, but unlike John Hutchins, she showed no surprise or anger at his words. She put on her coat, though, and picked up an expensive black leather briefcase.

"I'm afraid you'd be out of luck, Mr. Osborne. My son Ricky gave that gun to me several years ago as a Mother's Day gift. We'd had some break-ins in the neighborhood. I do not, however, approve of guns. I took self defense classes as my protection, and I never even took the gun out of the box. I asked Ricky to dispose of it, and haven't seen it since."

"And how did he dispose of it? Where is it now?" Sam asked.

"Why does this matter, Mr. Osborne? I got that rather unpleasant gift several years ago. I'm afraid I have no idea where it's gotten to," Anna Mae stepped outside the door, motioning for Sam to follow, and then pulled the door closed behind them.

"I'm just trying to follow up, ma'am. Someone took a shot at Casey just before this storm, and the police had very little time after the shooting to investigate. Casey has hired me to look into all this."

Anna Mae turned from her task of locking her front door.

"I'm not sure what you're referring to in regards to Casey. She certainly didn't share this with me. But if you're concerned about that gun, I'll call Ricky when I get to the office." She began walking towards the red Honda Civic in the driveway, extracting other keys from her purse as she went.

But Sam did not let her off the hook so easily. He followed her and stood next to the driver's side door while he took out his notebook and flipped through its pages.

"I'll ask Ricky about the gun," Sam said, making a note. "Perhaps he recalls what he did with it. I, do, however, have some other questions, such as what other types of vehicles do you drive besides this car, and do you recall where you were on January 13 at four p.m., January 27 at two and on September 16 of last year?"

Anna Mae raised her eyebrows. "Why?" she asked. "Am I under suspicion for something myself? Are those the dates of Casey's other accidents? I don't understand these questions." Her face relaxed then and, still looking at Sam, she pushed her key-less entry to open the car door and turned to accomplish that task.

Sam cleared his throat. "Mrs. Lewis. I know that none of you who know Casey believe the incidents she has reported are murder attempts. But it won't hurt for you to cooperate with me and the police in looking into this. And there has been a fourth attempt—"

At his words, Anna Mae's head snapped up and back towards Sam, "A fourth incident? What do you mean?" She straightened her shoulders and turned her body towards Sam.

"I'll let Casey fill you in on that. I'll be going with her this afternoon to fill out a police report. But for now, I'm just trying to get started with a few verifications. Can you tell me where you were on those dates?" He repeated the dates for her.

"Well, September 16 was a long time ago. But I guess you're in luck with all three of those dates. On Wednesdays, I'm at my hairdressers from two to four-thirty for my hair and nails. And most times I also get a facial," she said. "You can check with Elsie Gordon at Elsie's salon. As far as vehicles, this is Ricky's Honda. It drives better in the snow than my Mercedes."

Sam looked towards the house. "Can I talk to Ricky then, Anna Mae?"

"Ricky's not home right now, but I can have him call you. I don't think he's going to remember specific dates. He doesn't exactly keep an appointment book."

The car door was open. Anna Mae got in. She started the car and hesitated.

"Will there be anything else, Mr. Osborne? I'm sure Casey will tell you that I had nothing whatsoever to do with trying to hurt her. Even though she is Helen's daughter, I've shown her nothing but compassion and concern," Anna Mae's eyes were turned toward the windshield—unreadable to Sam.

"We'll talk later," he said, and he shut Anna Mae's door for her.

And maybe you can tell me why you know off the top of your head September 16 of six months ago was a Wednesday.

CHAPTER TWENTY-THREE

Danny sat on the loveseat by himself, watching Casey on her computer. Her long blond hair was gathered up in a ponytail, one escaped tendril falling across her face. He doubted she even noticed the escapee. Her attention was totally concentrated on the monitor.

Danny smiled, taking in the sight before him. Her brow was drawn up in thought about whatever topic she was researching. She was dressed in a soft pink blouse buttoned almost to the neck, and crisp brown pants. Casey's glasses rested on the end of her nose so that she could see both the keyboard and the computer screen. Danny thought she looked like a librarian, but one that most men would find absolutely delicious, with her sharp facial features and puckered lips. His fingers itched to grab the band that held her hair back and pull, letting the rest of the soft blond tresses free.

He was just about to tease her about the librarian image when she looked over and exclaimed, "I thought so—you can get a high school degree from a school in Lancaster using the internet. It's a study-at-home program for moms and dads who home school. How long it takes depends on how soon you feel you can take the required tests—it's not reliant on completing the actual courses."

The smile on Danny's face faltered. He tilted his head as if to take in her words.

"And how much does it cost?" Danny asked.

She turned away from the computer and looked directly at him. "Why does that even matter? You know I have plenty of money."

Danny's smile disappeared completely. He said nothing, but bent his head down, studying the clenched hands in his lap.

"How much does it cost, Casey?"

"Danny, goodness. What are you afraid of? That I will become your sugar-mama?" She chuckled at the thought. But when she peered at him closely, she saw how rigid his body had become.

"There's a yearly fee of about three hundred dollars to enroll, then some of the courses have materials or book costs, depending on what you're studying. But you may be able to test out of some of these classes by taking GED exams, Danny."

He still would not look at her.

"Danny, for goodness sakes. You can easily pay for these courses out of the money you'll be earning as a bodyguard. Let me pay for the fee upfront for this first one, and you can repay me with interest if you want."

He rolled his shoulders back and forth, unclenched his hands, and finally looked at her.

"You do realize, Casey, that while $300 may not be much to you, I've never had that amount of money at one time in my life. I do not want to be obligated to you in any way. Schooling can wait until I have made enough money."

He got up then and left the room.

Casey sat for a few minutes, stung by Danny's dismissal. She'd just been trying to help him. How could he not see the importance of schooling if he was going to get along in life? Maybe she had misjudged him. She thought he'd just been a victim of a broken foster system and cruel foster parents to end up on the streets. But maybe having someone like Gus watching out for him all those years had held him back from learning to make his own way in the world.

And who am I to judge? I've relied on others my whole life.

Outside the library, the storm that had been brewing for the last hour and a half suddenly broke. The snow that had blanketed the area turned to slush. Warmer weather hit, and the snow faded to many piles of dirty gray within forty-eight hours after it stopped falling. The temperatures had gone from freezing to unseasonably high. The skies this morning had turned ominously dark, and this time, when the clouds gave forth—rain, not snow or sleet, was the result.

The lightning flash and thunder clap were close together, startling Casey out of her thoughts. She hadn't even noticed when the downpour began.

Casey rolled to the window and drew back the curtain. Although it was only eleven in the morning, it looked more like twilight, it was so dark outside. She turned from the window and returned to her desk, but instead of staring at the computer, she sat staring at the shellacked surface of the oversize desk. Her gaze wandered to where Danny had been sitting.

She was picturing the hours the two had spent side by side on that loveseat, talking about books they'd read, the significance of certain historical events, how they felt about the people in their lives and what had happened to them both.

This time, when thunder hit, it was several seconds after the lightning flash.

The boom brought her out of her daze.

She smiled slightly and shook her head, then looked at the ceiling. "Okay. Okay, Gus. I'll give him time. I don't know your Danny well yet, but I know his heart is in the right place," she whispered.

An hour was all Danny needed. He found Casey in the dining room, munching on the sandwich Sarah had made. The rain hadn't stopped completely, but it had subsided to a low rhythmic patter.

When Danny sat in a chair at her side, Casey didn't look at him, but she picked up a sandwich half and held it in his direction.

He took the sandwich and began chewing. After several moments, he broke the silence.

"I'm sorry Casey. I know you're only looking out for me. I promise to consider your offer. I just think we need to concentrate on your other problem—who's trying to harm you. This guy has missed four times and must be desperate by now. I want nothing more than to keep you safe. But I think it's also time for me to take some action outside this house."

Casey studied his face, wondering what he was getting at.

"I want to help more, Casey. I want to give you back your life, and I want to find this guy."

"But what can you do, Danny, that Sam isn't doing?"

Danny pushed his chair away from the table and stood.

"I can be the chauffeur you keep saying I am, as well as your bodyguard. I just spoke with Sarah and Joseph, and Sarah has offered to teach me to drive. We're going out for my first lesson if you feel safe with just Joseph for awhile. I don't think it will take me long to learn the road rules. And I did some driving on those summers Gus and I spent at the lake. I think with just a few lessons, I can get my license. Once I have my license, you and I can go out together, and maybe I can help with the investigation."

Casey took his hand and squeezed.

"I'm sure Detective Osborne is working hard on discovering who it is, and we'll be filing more information with the police tomorrow," Casey reassured him. "I'm nervous, too. I want to get on with living and stop fearing dying. But I'll be fine alone for a while with Joseph."

After Sarah gave Danny his first driving lesson, he asked her to let him off downtown at Sam's office. Sarah had some shopping to do and promised to pick him back up in half-an-hour.

Sam greeted the young man with a handshake and offer of coffee. Danny and Sam sat for awhile discussing what was happening with Casey. Sam wasn't one hundred percent convinced the boy was as innocent as he seemed, but the detective hadn't been able to dig up any criminal background. And Danny seemed genuinely concerned about Casey's safety and eager to help. In fact, Sam suspected there was more than concern for an employer behind Danny's efforts.

"I've been thinking a lot about the motive, Sam. I know that Ricky stands to gain a lot from Richard's estate if Casey is out of the way so if you look at it purely from that angle, he seems like the most likely murderer."

Sam nodded.

"But it almost seems too obvious, and I've never trusted something that seems like a sure bet," Danny continued.

And you're smart not to, Sam thought.

"What if this has nothing to do with a chunk of money? What if it has to do with that audit—or maybe the company itself?"

You took the words right out of my mouth.

CHAPTER TWENTY-FOUR

Three cups of coffee after Danny's departure, Sam put on his rain coat and prepared to venture out into the now mild weather to seek out Ricky and Ginger. He had called around and arranged to meet them both at Ginger's apartment, which was only a few blocks from Sam's office.

Sam decided to tackle the short distance on foot. The walk would do him good, clear his head of the many details that crowded his brain when he was in the middle of an investigation.

Ginger opened the door to her apartment, and the five-foot-six-inch Sam had to look up to see her face. Her light red hair circled a face that lacked the sharp features of her half sister Casey, but Sam found it interesting for its many angles and for the bright green eyes that contrasted with the hair.

He glanced around the contemporary apartment, contrasting it with the grandeur of both the Lewis mansion and Anna Mae's costly home, not to mention the coldness of the Hutchins home and the slightly dingy feel of the Stone house. Ginger's place was filled with modern, but plush furniture—a cherry-red and bright-yellow, flowered sofa and matching chairs. The floors were hardwood, the walls painted a pale yellow and adorned with modern paintings.

Ricky was sitting in one of the side chairs next to the couch, one leg dangling over the chair's arm.

Sam couldn't quite figure Ricky out. He'd met him at a fundraiser last year that the young man attended with his mother. He'd spent a few moments in the group of people Ricky had been talking to—mostly young men and a few women who dressed like they had money and talked like they had fortunes. Their conversation was centered around horse racing, tennis and their busy social calendars.

Sam's initial impression about Ricky had been that, even though Ricky was twenty-seven, he acted like a little boy with bad manners who had no trouble laughing at his own jokes, but had little interest in anyone but himself. *Spoiled* was the word Sam had come up with.

Ricky was slender and wiry—in good shape from all that tennis, Sam thought. The young man had closely cropped, neat brown hair and a toothy smile. His height matched Ginger's and his blunt features and muscular arms kept him from being effeminate.

While the boy was friendly enough, Sam felt Ricky's true personality was never close to the surface. It was almost as if he practiced looking relaxed and manly, but at heart, he was something else.

"Well, hello, old chap. Got a big mystery that involves us, dear man?" Ricky chirped. Sam cringed inwardly at the fake British-accent, but smiled nonetheless.

"I explained on the phone the purpose of my visit. I have a few questions regarding what's happening with Casey," Sam said.

"Oh, you mean that shooting thing a couple weeks ago," Ricky said, his voice now his own. "Casey told me about it right after it happened, but I thought the police concluded it was a stray bullet. Don't know what she was doing in that questionable neighborhood, anyway."

Guess Casey isn't close enough to Ricky to share her love of theater, Sam thought. But Ricky had to have known about the other incidents since his mother had already dismissed them as accidents.

"You have some questions for me, too?" Ginger asked as she curled her lean body into a huge chair that matched the one Ricky was occupying.

"I have questions for both of you actually," Sam replied. "I need to ask you about the other attempts on Casey's life." Sam noticed a quick glance between the two.

They said in unison, "Other attempts?"

Sam ignored the question. He withdrew his old faithful notebook and flipped to a page.

"Let's start with you Ricky. Do you own or drive a silver or gray SUV?"

Ricky's face screwed up in confusion. "Mom has a Mercedes GL450. But why are you asking me questions you know the answer to? Mom said you'd been to the house. You know I drive both that SUV and my red Honda." He swung his leg back over the arm chair and sat up a little straighter.

Sam cleared his throat and continued.

"Where were you on Wednesday, January 13th, at four p.m., and on Wednesday, January 27th, at two p.m.? And where were you on September 16th of last year?"

"Come on now, you have to be kidding. How can you possibly expect me to remember exactly where I was last fall? Can anybody really recall where they were a week or two ago at a certain time?" Ricky asked.

Sam frowned at the sarcastic note in Ricky's voice. But he looked up and asked, "I am investigating more than the shooting, Mr. Lewis. I'm investigating several attempts on Casey's life, including one that took place during the blizzard. I'm taking Casey in to file a report on this latest attempt, and you're going to be answering to the police eventually, I'm sure. So you may as well answer a few questions for me as well."

"Okay. Okay," Ricky said as he put his hands up palms out. He then put those palms on the chair arms, pushed, and rose. "I don't believe her accidents were attempts on her life, but I can probably tell you where I was on the days you asked about. Let me go check my calendar. Maybe I can figure it out."

He left the room, and Sam turned to Ginger, "I'll need to know your whereabouts, too—on January 13th, January 27th, last September 16th."

"You really think someone is trying to kill Casey?" Ginger said, her emerald eyes focused on Sam's face.

"Do you have reason to doubt it?"

Ginger got up from her perch, stretched, yawned, and drawled, "Casey does like the attention. Look, Mr. Osborne. You have to realize that I grew up in a household where everything that girl said was golden. My mom and her dad, my step-father Richard, adored her—spoiled her rotten. She could do no wrong. We aren't exactly close as siblings go."

"And why is that?" Sam asked.

"When she didn't get the attention she thought she deserved, she created a reason—a scraped knee, an injured ego. You name it. Casey knew how to play the mom-dad card. Ricky and I were just seconds—another mom for him, another dad for me. Casey was the center of their universe."

Ginger's face closed suddenly, and she turned away and walked over to the white desk in the corner of the room. Grabbing a leather datebook, she returned to her chair and once again curled her body into it.

She flipped through the pages, looking for the dates Sam had mentioned.

"Well, I'm sorry if someone is really out to get her," she said without looking up from the book. "But it isn't me. And don't ask me to feel sorry for her. There's no love lost between us, but I wouldn't hurt her.

"It appears," Ginger continued, "on Wednesday, January 13th, I was in Pittsburgh with Ricky at a comic book convention."

She looked up at Sam then, and he was surprised at the animation he saw in her face.

"Ricky is very much into comics. He writes them, you know. And I'm thinking about illustrating them for him."

Sam looked around the room, noting the oil paintings on the wall. "Are any of these your work, or do you collect as well?" he asked. "They're quite good."

Ginger looked pleased by the compliment. "These are all mine, Mr. Osborne. But I'm really better with caricatures and people pictures. I took a few classes, thought of going to art school, but I don't really have the money, now that we're being cut off from Dad Lewis's estate. Typical of old Dad Lewis, though. Everything always revolved around Casey. I wasn't really surprised when I found out she inherits a fortune at twenty-one while Ricky and I are out on our butts."

"You've had eight years to go to school," Sam pointed out. "Eight years of trust funds with money coming in. Why didn't you go to school when you had it?"

Ginger's face crumpled just a bit. "Fifty thousand dollars a year sounds like a lot. But when you're young and you're foolish, it goes pretty fast. I didn't really think about school until recently."

She looked down at the calendar again. "I have nothing marked on January 27 or last September. I probably just stayed home and drew."

Her eyes returned to Sam's face. "On January 27, though, which was just, what like a week and a half ago, I think Ricky was out with friends."

Why does Ginger keep tabs on Ricky's whereabouts? Sam thought. *They certainly are close.*

Ricky came back with an iPad in hand. "Nothing for last September, but it seems I was out of town on the 13th," he said. "There was a big comic book convention in Pittsburgh and I left early in the day to go to it. Took Ginger with me. We didn't get back until the next day."

"And the 27th?" Sam said.

"Went to the races with friends. Want their names?"

"Yes," Sam said, "and the name of the hotel in Pittsburgh."

After he'd recorded the relevant information in his notebook, Sam put down his pen and addressed them both.

"Do either of you have any idea who might want to harm Casey?" Instead of looking at Sam, though, the two looked at each other. Ricky was the one to answer. But first he sat down again in the chair and swung his leg back over the arm. He put his hands behind his head, splaying his elbows outwards in a stretch. Then he turned toward Sam.

"I know Casey believes there is some grand plot out there to take her out of the picture because of the will. But that's just Casey being Casey. She's a drama queen, and she hasn't had much practice in the last few years. She's got the moola to hire a detective, and if it makes her feel better, so be it. But no—I don't believe for a minute there is anyone out to get her. Certainly, Ginger and I are not trying to kill our sister!"

Sam rose then, put his pen in his pocket and picked up his notebook. He'd bring up the fourth incident later—after the police report was filed and the warrants were served. But he had to wonder why neither of them had even asked what the fourth attempt was.

CHAPTER TWENTY-FIVE

After putting together a ham, cheese and rye sandwich for supper that night, Sam sat at his kitchen table and ate slowly, stretching his mental muscles to prepare for a marathon session with his notes. He had scheduled a trip to the police station with Danny and Casey to file a report the next afternoon, and he wanted to put the facts together in his head and decide what he could share.

When the last crumbs of his sandwich were gone, he went into his study, pulled out his files with details of the case, and powered up his computer, studied his notes and what he'd stored on the computer, then went to his ever-present bulletin board. He didn't rely as heavily on computers in his process as most of today's detectives did. He'd been forced to learn the fundamentals, and there was no denying the usefulness of the Internet for research. But he still used a bulletin board and a large pad of paper to make lists and draw lines connecting the facts of the case. He needed that visual representation—the same method he'd used for the last quarter century—to put it all together.

He took out a pad of paper and at the top of each page printed the name of a suspect, then under each name, he put *motive, and alibis during attempts.* Under alibis he put the dates of each attempt on Casey's life.

This accomplished, he went back into the kitchen and opened a bottle of beer, carried it back into the study, and began a process that had solved many mysteries in his time as a detective. On each piece of paper, he wrote what he suspected to be true and what was a proven point. Under John Hutchins's and Reggie Stone's, he wrote, *Cooking the books,* then followed it with a question mark and added, *Audit would reveal.*

Sam had dug as far as he could into company affairs, but he had no legal reason for gaining access to the actual accounting numbers. He'd need help from his friend Robert McCoy for that, and he wasn't sure yet what he was looking for. On paper, the company appeared to be thriving. Two incidents, however, had led him to question the actions of the company's top executives.

The first was an interview he'd conducted earlier that day with one of the company employees. Sam had talked by phone to several employees whose names Casey had supplied— people who had worked for the company for a few years. Gertrude Tabias was one of those, a sixty-five-year-old former secretary for John Hutchins who had recently retired. Sam had visited her in person.

Sam had asked the gray-haired, thin woman what it had been like to work for the man and how John had gotten along with Casey.

"He never forgot a birthday," was the first thing that Gertrude, who was neatly dressed in blouse and skirt despite her retirement, came up with. She crossed her feet at the ankle and pulled both legs to one side.

When Sam pushed further, Gertrude admitted that John could be demanding, but that she expected nothing less of a boss with the load of responsibility that John carried.

"And how long did you work for Mr. Hutchins?"

"Five years and nine months. It would have been six if I hadn't retired when I did."

"And before that? Where did you work in the company?"

The woman's face suddenly pinched into a frown.

"I had one year with Anna Mae Lewis. That was all anyone ever worked for that woman. We called it 'serving time' at Lewis Pharmaceuticals. All of us girls in the secretarial pool have worked for her at one time or another. But she runs through assistants like panty hose."

The woman's face then relaxed.

"That's why it wasn't so bad with Mr. Hutchins. I'd done my time with Anna Mae, who can be a total, well, she's just very difficult to please. Mr. Hutchins required that I work long hours, but he always gave me extra time off when he did so. I didn't mind working nine-hour days early in the week because I had most Fridays half-days or completely off."

"I can see that would be an incentive," Sam said. "A lot of three-day weekends?"

"Yes. Fridays were payday as well as the day Mr. Hutchins balanced the books. He'd let me distribute the paychecks in the morning, but I usually got to go home by lunch."

Sam had looked up from his notes then. Gertrude sat perched on the edge of the arm chair, her legs still drawn back under her, sipping a cup of coffee. She'd offered a cup to

Sam, poured from an expensive-looking china set she'd explained was one of the birthday presents John Hutchins had given her.

Gertrude wasn't looking at Sam, but at his notebook resting on the coffee table as if she were trying to read his handwriting at the 90-degree angle. She put down her coffee cup.

"You didn't help Mr. Hutchins with the accounting?"

"Goodness no." Gertrude's tone rose just a notch. "Mr. Hutchins is a CPA. I'm just an assistant. What they used to call a secretary. I only handled his correspondence, telephone calls and other administrative tasks. He always said he didn't trust anyone else to get the numbers right."

"I see," Sam had mused. Gertrude uncrossed her legs then, straightened her skirt, crossed her legs in the opposite direction and picked up her coffee cup.

"So you never looked over the books, maybe to proofread them for him or to make adjustments he asked for?"

The woman had put her coffee cup down again, spilling a little of its contents on the fine bone china saucer.

"I didn't even have access to those computer records, Mr. Osborne. There was no need. It was not my job."

Sam had ended the interview shortly after that, noting in his book that John Hutchins had as expensive a taste in gifts as he had in living room furniture. Gertrude had been given a Coach handbag for an annual anniversary, a set of designer suitcases for Christmas, and a small pair of diamond studs for her sixty-fifth birthday/retirement party. The assistant had proudly listed his thoughtful gifts before clamming up when Sam started asking about the bookkeeping.

Sam added a note under John's name on the bulletin board.

Buying secretary's loyalty? Where is the money coming from?

Next up for the day, Sam met for lunch with an old friend and someone on whom he could depend on to get what he needed, such as being able to accompany the police officers serving warrants for Anna Mae and John Hutchins's homes. Lieutenant Robert McCoy and Sam had worked together when Sam was a member of the police force. They'd made detective around the same time and worked a few cases together. The fact that Sam was out on his own changed their relationship somewhat, but the two still shared many a meal together over the years, swapping what information they could and talking over cases they were investigating.

They met at their favorite watering hole and burger joint.

"I'll just have a green salad and maybe cook me a burger without a bun today. And no cheese, Trudy," Bob said to the waitress. She raised her eyebrows in response.

"I thought you looked like you dropped a few pounds, Bob," Sam said to his friend, "On a diet?"

"Kinda, though it's not official. The doc says if I'm going to enjoy my retirement years, the cholesterol has to come down. I ain't giving up Joe's burgers completely, though. Just cutting the carbs and hitting the gym. Already lost 10 pounds."

"Congratulations," Sam said. But he didn't let Bob's success keep him from ordering a bleu-cheese burger and fries.

After they had eaten and Sam had caught up on what each of Bob's kids was doing, they turned to Sam's case. The detective filled the ex-detective in on the latest developments, omitting the names. Sam asked if Bob knew anything about Lewis Pharmaceuticals.

"Lewis Pharmaceuticals, huh," Bob said, as he sat back in the cheap metal dining room chair. He knitted his fingers and rested them on the slight roll that remained on his abdomen.

Sam narrowed his eyes at his friend.

"You know something." It wasn't a question.

"And you know that if I did, I wouldn't give you specifics," Bob answered.

But Sam sat back in his own metal chair and smiled.

"Then tell me what you can't give me details about."

"I know that the local drug task force has discovered they need to be tracking down a new source of supply. It seems that drugs have been hitting the streets around here that aren't the usual street drugs, but things like the painkillers Demoral and hydrocodone and the ever popular Adderall, which is supposed to be for people with Attention Deficit Disorder, but is a popular drug among college students.

"They don't know exactly how it's being done, but the supplies the drug task force has been able to track down look like they've been re-manufactured—they don't have the required pill-name stamped on them or they've been put into new plastic capsules."

Sam's only comment was "Interesting." He knew the best way to get information out of his friend was not to press hard. He also knew that Lewis Pharmaceuticals had one of only two drug manufacturing plants in a 200-mile radius of Lancaster.

"Yeah—I'll say." Bob leaned forward over the table, and lowered his voice, even though no one was listening. "And I heard that lab analysis shows the drug contents seemed to be broken down somewhat—they aren't quite full strength when tested, as if they'd been around awhile, and they aren't cut with the usual fillers. They're not exactly sure what to make of it, but they think the originals might have been expired drugs. I guess they could have come from out-of-state or even out of this area, but the boys seemed to think it was the work of a gang around here that stays pretty close at hand."

Bob sat back and picked up his napkin, dabbing at his mouth though they had long since finished their meal. "Like I said, I can't tell you much more. But I will say that the boys in the gang that have been getting those drugs have to be getting help from someone with access to the right pharmaceuticals."

"Any ideas of who that someone might be?" Sam asked.

Bob shook his head, and Sam knew the fountain of data was about the run dry.

"You know I won't tell you that. But if I were investigating, I'd look at who had either the most expensive taste or the most bills to pay."

They both reached for the check then, but Sam got there first. He figured he owed his old friend a burger, even if it was plopped on top of a salad.

When he'd returned to the office, he spent the next hour and a half looking through what he'd learned about his suspects' credit backgrounds. It seemed Reggie Stone was up to his eyeballs in medical bills. Both John Hutchins and Anna Mae Lewis had expensive taste, which showed up on the amount of charging they did on their gold cards. But their credit remained good.

Of course, it could be that someone within the company that wasn't on his list of suspects was responsible for selling expired drugs, but the murder attempts and crime at the plant were too much of a coincidence. Sam didn't believe in coincidence.

CHAPTER TWENTY-SIX

Sarah is teaching me how to bake. I made these cookies myself," Casey said as she offered one to Sam.

Sam placed it on a china plate next to the cup of coffee Sarah had poured for him out of a delicate, flowered coffeepot. He noted that Danny, who was standing next to Casey's chair, took one of the cookies also, then squeezed Casey's shoulder and smiled.

Casey looked up at Danny, her eyes lighting up as if her newly appointed bodyguard and chauffeur had just told her she'd won a first-place ribbon at a county fair.

And the cookies truly were good: warm and soft with a hint of cinnamon. For just a moment, the snack took Sam's mind away from the purpose of his visit. But Sam's mind was never far from the case at hand and the fine bone china of his coffee cup brought him back into the room.

"How well do you know John Hutchins's background? From what I've found out, he came from a blue collar background; a father who worked at the mill before it closed, and a mother that passed away while John was in his teens."

Casey brushed a crumb from her lap. "I have never known John well enough to ask about his background. I knew he didn't come from wealthy parents—Daddy mentioned how far his ambition had taken him in the company. But you have to realize I was only a pre-teen when Daddy died, so to me, John has always just been the ambitious business professional."

Sam cleared his throat. "He seems to have accumulated quite a bit of wealth—more than his salary could account for. I thought maybe he came from a wealthy background, but he seems to be the only heir of a factory worker who never had much money. He's known around town as a big spender—he belongs to the local country club, drives an expensive car, and lavishes expensive gifts on his loyal employees."

Sam paused before adding, "He's also one of my main suspects. The bullet that was left in the tree came from a revolver that matches the make of guns that both John and Ricky own."

Casey tilted her head slightly and ran a hand over her blond hair. Danny, who had remained standing at her side, plopped down in a nearby armchair.

"So it could have been either one of them?" he asked.

"There's much more," Sam continued. "John was uncooperative when I asked to see his gun. I obtained permission to be included when a search warrant I arranged through a friend on the police force was served. I returned to his house the same day with several officers, who proceeded to do the search."

"He couldn't have been very happy about that!" Casey said.

"He wasn't home. I timed it that way. His housekeeper was not about to object to a warrant. I called to let John know, but the search was well on its way by then."

Sam took another bite of cookie. "Frankly, I did not expect the outcome of that search to be so fruitful."

Sam could feel the inquiring eyes of Casey, Danny, Sarah and Joseph.

"The warrant on Ricky's gun was not served. I had already asked Anna Mae, in a separate interview, about the firearm, which she said was lost a long time ago. But before the police had a chance to return with the warrant for Anna Mae and Ricky's home, we found the gun that was originally registered to Ricky—at John Hutchins's place during the search there."

Four sets of eyes widened at the news.

"Frankly, I was as surprised as you are. We found what we thought was John's gun in a desk drawer early in the search. But when John arrived, he took us straight to where he said his gun was—locked away in a bedroom safe. We walked away with two guns and found out later whose they were."

"But why?" Casey exclaimed. "Why would he have both guns, and what does John have to gain by my death?"

"I don't know exactly why he'd be involved, but I'm guessing the audit may reveal something John doesn't want to come out. As far as the second gun, he looked shocked when we showed it to him, and said he had no idea where it had come from. In the meantime, the police have nothing to hold him on, though they'll probably bring him in for questioning. Meanwhile, we've sent both guns to the lab to compare against the bullet and see if we can eliminate either."

Sam grabbed another cookie and sat back in his chair, "there's more," he said.

Danny and Casey turned towards each other. Danny smiled, then and took Casey's hand, but Casey just looked shaken. She turned back to Sam.

"Go on."

"It appears Lewis Pharmaceuticals may be part of an investigation into expired drugs being sold on the black market. The drugs are being repackaged and distributed by a local gang. I don't have confirmation on this yet— it's an ongoing investigation. Although I have someone who is keeping me as up to date as he can. Anyway, I think it's highly likely that John, Anna Mae, or maybe Reggie is selling the supply of expired drugs for profit on the street."

Casey's face whitened, and Sam gave her a moment to compose herself and let the information sink in while he flipped through his notes.

"I also did some checking on where everyone was during the attempts on your life. Of course, this is assuming that the would-be murderer is someone within your close circle.

"Everyone appears to have either been in town on September 16, or unable to remember back that far, but since we have no idea how that first 'accident' was set up or when, it doesn't really matter. As far as the day the car tried to mow you down, we have a pretty precise time, 4:00 p.m.

"Ricky and Ginger were both out of town at the time and too far away to have made it back, which doesn't mean they couldn't have hired someone. Meanwhile, there was a staff meeting at Lewis Pharmaceuticals that day at three, and John Hutchins and Reggie would have been there from three until whenever it ended. Since Lewis Pharmaceuticals is across town from the park, I'm not sure either of them could have made it in time to aim a car at you—though again, either could have hired someone."

Danny interrupted then, "And wouldn't Anna Mae also have been at that meeting?"

Good deduction. Sam turned to address his next remark to Danny.

"As it happens, she is not part of that staff meeting. As CEO, she apparently spends a good deal of time at the company, working late every night and most weekends. But that meeting is not something she attends; it's for the rest of the staff. She has a standing appointment at her salon every Wednesday from two until four, so she would have been there both that day and the day of the third attempt.

"And where was everyone else on January 27?" Casey asked.

"Ricky was at the races with friends for the day, which was confirmed by both Ginger and several of those friends. Ginger herself has no alibi. John was at work, but I've received no confirmation from anyone who remembers his presence during that exact time. Of course, he would have been at the staff meeting by three, but that gives him enough time to drive to the park and back."

"And Uncle Reg?" Casey asked, a tremor now present in her voice.

"He was at the doctor at two p.m. the day of the third attack. On the day of the car incident, Ellie hadn't been doing well, and she apparently had some sort of attack that landed her in the emergency room. The hospital confirmed that Reggie signed the papers for her admittance."

"What is your theory about this most recent attempt?" Joseph asked, "Who was able to make it out in a giant snowstorm and try to harm our Casey? Who would leave her, hurt on the floor, to die in such a terrible manner?"

"This one has me most troubled for that very reason," Sam said. "The snow was piled pretty deep—at least eighteen to twenty-four inches fell during the course of the evening. A car with four-wheel drive might have made it up the drive far enough. The assailant could have other transportation such as a snowmobile, or simply have trekked by foot to the area. Too much snow fell afterward to find any clear footprints. There did appear to be snowmobile tracks on the property, but many vehicles were out during and after the snowfall. We don't get that kind of fresh powder too often.

"We also don't know the exact time the assailant got into the house, but I found no traces of a break-in. Casey, you told me you had locked it up tight, so it has to be someone with access to a key."

"That means Ricky and Reggie," Casey said. Ricky had a key for his nights away from his mother and Reggie had always had a key, though he rarely used it.

"And Joseph and Sarah of course," Sam added.

Both of Casey's caregivers turned to glare in Sam's direction.

"Relax, I know you were on your way to Sarah's sister. You couldn't have been here and made it there when you did. I'm just laying out the facts. Did you take your keys with you?"

Sarah and Joseph looked at each other, and then Joseph withdrew a set of keys from his pocket and laid them on the table.

"My house key is on the chain with the car keys."

Sarah's forehead wrinkled in thought, and then she rose from the couch.

"And mine is in a basket in the foyer—under several pairs of gloves we keep there. I take the key if I'm going out without Joseph, or Casey grabs it if she's going out for a stroll." Sarah left the room and returned a few moments later.

"Whew. It's still there," she said as she sat back down and deposited a single key on a chain onto the coffee table.

"That doesn't mean, however, that the would-be killer didn't grab the key the night of incident and return it later," Sam pointed out.

Casey sighed deeply then and sat back.

"It doesn't sound like we're any closer to finding out who it is. They all have possible motives. They all have alibis for some of the events. How will we ever narrow it down?"

Sam's kind brown eyes found Casey's and stuck. Her expression reflected the disappointment the investigation had been so far.

"Let's start by filing that police report this afternoon on the latest attempt. It will give them someplace to start looking. I'm working on a few theories, Casey, and my friend at the police headquarters, Bob McCoy, is the best there is. We'll find our man—or woman."

CHAPTER TWENTY-SEVEN

Sam, Casey, Danny, and Bob McCoy were gathered in Bob's office. Casey looked drained. They'd been there for almost three hours, filing the official police report and going over the details of what Sam had learned, as well as other details that affected the case. While Casey was glad the police were now on her side, she'd spent a good deal of time at the beginning of the process convincing the detective who initially interviewed them that Danny was not the villain. The fact that Danny had showed up in the middle of a snowstorm just in time to save her from freezing to death was hard for a police officer to swallow.

However, like Sam, Bob McCoy seemed to reach the conclusion that Danny had no motive and no previous connection to Casey or the Lewis family. Danny also had no police record, had not attempted to harm Casey or steal anything from the house, and had probably saved her life.

McCoy and the other officers changed direction in their questions and began to go over with Casey who else might want to harm her and with Sam, what the detective had found in his research.

Sam wasn't ready to share his theories, but unlike some private investigators, he believed he had the most to gain by sharing facts as much as he could. He filled police in on the provisions of the will and the roles each of the people closest to Casey played in Lewis Pharmaceuticals. He also showed police what he'd found the day before when he took a construction inspector out to the fallen timber that used to be the walk out.

That last task had not an easy one since the snow of the blizzard had been replaced by rain and mud. The mud was so intense, Casey had hired a local expert climber to brave the steep drop off using climbing equipment that would not allow an accident. The climber took a camera down the cliff, and snapped pictures of what remained of the timber. If Casey, Sam and the police felt there was anything to be found, they would return with a crew later and bring up the fallen structure. For now, Sam had wanted to see if anything could be spotted.

In the police office, Sam pointed at a piece of wood that had a deep cut in one side and two smaller pieces that had jagged edges.

"The inspector says those marks on the wood that's still intact could well be made from a saw. Although this piece did not crack through, it's greatly weakened. He also said these other two pieces look like they could have been part of the same type of fortification lumber, but that they had splintered. Based on the plans I got from the project builder, he said all of these could be the support beams under the main platform, but that he was just speculating based on their size. When the inspector looked at where they were on the project plan, he said that it was possible someone in good shape could have leaned over the sides or had support and climbing ropes to help reach these particular beams. The builder speculated that, using a curved saw with a good handle, a person could have weakened the whole structure by weakening those supports."

Bob McCoy scratched his head.

"Doesn't seem like a very sure-fire way of killing someone," he said.

"Agreed. But since Casey is the only one who ever uses these structures, it definitely could have been an attempt that would likely be written off as an accident."

Bob rubbed his chin with one hand and looked up at his long-time friend. "But freezing her to death. This person has to be one cruel dude."

Sam held his friend's gaze.

"I think whoever it is, is getting pretty desperate. Attempts one, two, and three did not work and he or she may have just seen this storm as an opportunity. Casey didn't report any of this until a week before the storm when she filed a report on the gunshots and you had just started your investigation. The would-be killer may not even know about that report or the fact that a bullet was found."

Bob sat back in his chair. "Well I bet the killer is really frantic now and maybe not thinking as clearly." He looked at Danny.

"You'd better keep a close eye on Casey, Mr. Jones. We'll continue the investigation we began before the storm, and I intend to head that investigation up, but we don't have a lot to go on at this point and her birthday is only a few weeks away."

CHAPTER TWENTY-EIGHT

Casey was going stir crazy. Danny would not let her out of his sight. While she loved his conversation most of the time, they had been stuck together in the house for almost two weeks. She had suggested several outings, but Danny wouldn't hear of it. He'd continued his driving lesson, but she had only been to the police station and back.

Casey sighed deeply and picked up her book. She supposed he was right. The police were investigating and hopefully (and with Sam's help) would come up with some answers soon. The safest place for her right now was in her own home. But she'd never been much of a television person, and you could only play so many games of solitaire or Monopoly.

She looked over at Danny, curled up in the armchair with his own book. One stray strand of his dark hair kept falling into his eyes. Without thinking, he kept pushing it back so he could see the words on the page.

Casey put her book in her lap. "You need a haircut."

Danny's head snapped up. Casey laughed at the startled look on his face.

"You really could use a haircut, Danny," she said in a softer tone.

Danny ran both hands through his hair.

"I'm not going to a barber shop, Casey."

Casey sighed. *Wouldn't life be blessed when they could live normal lives?*

"Then I'll do it," she said. She started wheeling towards the kitchen, and Danny followed.

"You know how to cut hair?" he asked.

"Nope," Casey said without turning around. Once she'd reached the kitchen and grabbed a towel and scissors, she turned to him and asked, "Do you really care? When was the last time you got your hair cut?" she asked.

Danny laughed softly.

"I guess the last time I had access to scissors. I try to keep up with it, but with this storm, my trip, some work I had before I left, I guess it's been a while."

They returned to the library, which had become their favorite room. Casey transferred to the armchair, and Danny sat on the floor at Casey's feet. The only sound for the next twenty minutes was a snip here and a clip there, but the near silence didn't bother either of them. They were as comfortable not talking as they were in sharing their thoughts. The scent of Sarah's delicious bran muffins wafted in from the kitchen, adding to the atmosphere of tranquility and hominess.

The domestic scene was interrupted by the shrill of the phone. Neither Danny nor Casey attempted to pick it up, however, because both Joseph and Sarah were at home.

Sarah came into the library, her left hand encased in an oven mitt, the right clutching a handset. Her brows rose inquisitively at the sight of Danny on the floor, a towel around his shoulders, but she smiled before handing the phone over to Casey. "It's Reggie Stone."

Danny got up and retreated to the loveseat and his book, the towel still around his shoulders. In the first few days of his work as her bodyguard, he left the room whenever she got a call. But Casey had urged him to stay. She had no secrets or need for privacy.

"Uncle Reg? How's Ellie? Oh—I'm sorry. I hope she feels better soon."

Then Casey was silent as she took in whatever Reggie was saying. Soon, she began to nod her head, then murmur "Mmm. Hmm." And "That makes sense."

Finally, she said. "Yes. Of course. I can see how that might be important. March 15? No, of course, I have nothing scheduled. It's the day before my birthday. Seems like a good way to celebrate. I'm sure Daddy would have been delighted. Are you having it catered, then?"

A few minutes later, she said, "Of course I'll be there," before pushing the button to disconnect.

Casey sat thinking for a moment before putting the phone aside and looking over at Danny. What she saw startled her out of her private thoughts. Danny had removed the towel and was holding it tightly in both hands, his head bowed. His whole body looked tense.

"Danny?"

He looked up at her then, his gaze steady and questioning.

"You'll be where?" he said. "It sounds like a party."

Casey's brow wrinkled in confusion.

"Daddy bought the business twenty-five years ago this month, and Lewis Pharmaceuticals was born shortly thereafter. The company is having an anniversary gala that night—inviting local politicians, the media, retired employees. Giving out some awards. Since I'm taking over ownership on my birthday, Anna Mae and Reggie, the other two partners, thought it would be a good idea if I were there. Good PR for the company, Anna Mae said."

Danny got up to pace. He stopped and turned to address her. "I don't think so."

Casey's eyes widened.

"Excuse me? You don't think so *what*?"

Danny stood in front of her, and she had to look up to see his face.

"Whoever is trying to kill you is very likely to be at that party."

Casey put her hand to her throat.

"Yes. So? It's not like they're going to try anything at a big gathering like that."

Suddenly Danny seemed huge to Casey. She was used to seeing him at her level because they were doing something together, talking, reading, playing a game. He was usually seated, sometimes on the floor at her feet. Now, he seemed to loom over her.

"Casey." His deep voice bounced against the walls. "I can't keep you safe in a room with hundreds of people. You can't go to a party!"

Casey looked away from him, her eyes seeking the familiarity of her wheelchair.

"A party is not important, Casey. It's just a bunch of people with a reason to be together. You're not even part of the company yet."

She grabbed the chair's handle and began to pull it towards her, forcing Danny to move from in front of her. With her other hand, she steadied the wheelchair at a ninety-degree angle from where she sat, then used both hands on the arms and seat of the chair she was in to push herself up. She scooted her rear towards the wheel chair and plopped down onto its canvas seat. She had not said a word.

"Casey. There's time to be part of this company if you want—later. After the killer is found. But it's too dangerous for you to go right now. You really *can't* go to a party. I won't allow it."

Casey finally looked back up at Danny, and then wheeled backward so she could see his face a little better.

"You do not tell me what I can and cannot do, Danny Jones." She turned the chair and began to wheel away.

But Danny had the advantage. He grabbed an arm and stopped her progress. "Listen to me—" Her face made him stop. Her eyes were narrowed, her breathing coming in short gasps. Her lips were drawn in a straight line.

"Let. My. Chair. Go."

Danny took a step back and held up his hands, palms out. His body seemed to react to her anger by heating up. His face reddened, and his hands clenched into fists.

Casey resumed wheeling and left the room.

Joseph answered Sam's knock at the door. The caregiver ushered him inside and motioned towards the living room.

"I'm not sure where Casey is at the moment, but I'll go find her." he said.

Sam knew the moment he walked into the living room that something was wrong. Danny was pacing back and forth like a caged animal in front of the giant fireplace, deep in thought.

"Have I come at a bad time?"

Danny hadn't even noticed his arrival. He swung his head around and appeared to be adjusting his focus to the here and now. He cleared his throat, then crossed the remaining short distance and took Sam's hand in greeting.

"I don't know. I'm not exactly sure. Well—I guess so." He plopped into the armchair and put his head in his hands. Sam gave Danny a moment to collect himself. When Danny looked up, his brows were raised, and a scowl spoiled his handsome face.

"I'm not used to fighting with people, Sam. Gus—the guy I told you about—was a father figure. He didn't allow me to fight, even with him. In later years, when I was taking care of him, we had our share of disagreements, but by then he was too sick to argue."

Sam nodded his head, and sat down on the sofa. "You and Casey had a fight."

"Yes. I think so. I got very upset with her. I may have raised my voice some." Danny put his head back in his hands, then sat up and ran both palms over his hair.

Sam noticed the haircut, but said nothing. Normally, the detective would have excused himself and left. But Danny's look of pain kept Sam rooted to the spot.

"Lewis Pharmaceuticals is having a party to celebrate their twenty-fifth anniversary right before Casey's birthday. Casey is insisting on going."

Sam kept silent. Danny's eyes turned to appeal to Sam.

"There'll be hundreds of people there, the general public, the media. Every one of the people affected by the will and the hand-over of the company.

Still Sam said nothing.

"I can't keep her safe under those circumstances. I don't even know if I can keep her safe *period.*"

Danny stood and resumed his pacing.

"I'm in over my head here, Sam. I'm not a trained bodyguard. I can't do this. I can't lose her." He seemed to surprise himself then with what he'd said, and he sat back down in the chair.

Sam rose. He walked over to Danny and laid a hand on the young man's shoulder.

"It's been a tense couple of days, Danny. You're cooped up in this house, trying to figure things out. You'll work this out, too."

"I can't lose her, Sam," Danny repeated, letting the words really sink in this time.

Sam thought for moment, and then withdrew his hand.

"I'm on my way to meet up with police. The investigation into the expired drugs has gone into full-steam. Officer McCoy and his force have expanded the original warrant for Anna Mae's house to look for evidence relating to the expired drugs. They have warrants pending for other key employees' homes as well. But since I'm helping with the investigation on the murder attempts, they're allowing me to observe this first search. They can't let you into the house, but why don't you come along for the ride. It might take your mind off things for a while, or at least give you some time away from the house. I'll bring you back in an hour or so."

Danny was shaking his head.

"Sarah and Joseph are here with her now," Sam said. "They watch her as closely as you do. Give *her* some time alone to think."

Danny looked over at Sam, the pain of love evident in his eyes.

"A couple of hours?" Danny asked.

"Sarah and Joseph will keep her safe," Sam said.

CHAPTER TWENTY-NINE

S am didn't try to make conversation on the fifteen minute drive from Casey's home to Anna Mae's house. Because Danny was not allowed in the house, the detective left the younger man alone in the car across the street from the home.

Danny watched as officers combed the outside of the house, looking for an entry point. They found an unlocked back door and were inside. Then he'd lost interest in the goings on. He sat staring at his own hands. He didn't even notice that the rain had finally stopped, the air was warmer; the sun shone more brilliantly than it had since before the blizzard. His thoughts were trapped with him inside the car.

What business do I have trying to be someone's bodyguard? I couldn't keep Gus safe. I have no idea how to keep Casey safe.

Danny sighed deeply and rested an elbow on the console, then put his head in his hand.

If Casey gets killed, it will be my fault. I don't have any training. I don't even know what to watch out for.

Although Sam tried to reassure Danny that she was okay in the big house with Joseph and Sarah, Danny didn't even want to leave Casey there. He knew he had been slowly driving her crazy, checking the windows and doors every few hours, finding reasons why they didn't have to leave the house. Much of the last few days had been like the first days of the snowstorm—reading side-by-side or talking—but it hadn't been enough. He'd felt like a caged animal, and he'd caged Casey in with him.

Casey should have hired the experienced guy Sam suggested. I never should have accepted her offer. I only took this job because I need the money and love having a place to stay for awhile.

But Danny shook his head and smiled a crooked smile, and rubbed it away with his hand. He knew that wasn't exactly true. He'd taken the job to stay close to this blond woman with the sea-green eyes whose approval he sought more than anyone ever in his life—even his beloved Gus.

Gus, old friend. What do I do? Can I somehow learn how to keep her alive?

A knock on the window interrupted his thoughts. Sam motioned for Danny to roll down the window.

"They found nothing in the house that ties Anna Mae or Ricky to a crime. I guess that doesn't surprise me. Anna Mae seems too clever a woman to leave evidence about in her own home if she is somehow involved in all this."

Sam glanced back at the house. The garage door was open, the officers were now pouring through the few storage bins on shelving and a file cabinet in the double-car structure.

Suddenly, Danny sat up. He rolled the window the rest of the way down and leaned out as if doing so would allow him to see better. Then he came to his senses, opened the car door and got out to lean his rear against the car and watch, standing side by side with Sam. Sam sensed the young man's tension and looked over at the boy, then back at the garage. Without saying anything, the detective realized what Danny was seeing. A bright red snowmobile parked against the far wall of the garage.

"Lots of people have snowmobiles," Sam said.

The two men were silent then, watching as the police pulled more bins from the shelves. One officer was going through the pockets of a snowsuit that hung behind the snowmobile. He pulled something out of one pocket, and Sam and Danny realized at the same moment—the moment the officer flipped it open and pushed a button—what it was. They looked at each other, and Danny said it first.

"A cell phone. Sam—why would Anna Mae keep a cell phone in the garage? Sam—don't you have Casey's cell phone number in your phone?"

"Yup," Sam said as he opened his own phone. "But it's been two weeks. The battery surely will have died—unless maybe it's been off this whole time."

Sam dialed the number. Neither man was surprised when the officer answered.

After a short conversation with the policeman, Sam pushed his phone's end call button.

"That gives them enough to bring Anna Mae and Ricky in for questioning. They'll have some explaining to do as to why they have Casey's cell." Sam couldn't help but be pleased. He'd come along on this drug bust because he suspected Anna Mae was somehow involved.

Ricky was also high on his list, but he'd done some talking to the corporate lawyers. The CEO of Lewis Pharmaceuticals had almost as much to gain by Casey's death as Ricky because with the younger woman out of the way, Anna Mae would be completely in charge of the company. Her own son would be majority stockholder.

Sam's phone rang, "Oh god. When was that? She's where? O.K. That's only a couple blocks from here. Yea, we'll be there as soon as we can."

Sam's face was pale, and Danny suddenly felt like someone had walked up and slapped his face hard. Something had happened to Casey. Danny felt it in his bones.

"What. What is it!"

Sam turned slowly to Danny.

"She's alive, Danny. She's in the hospital—"

"I knew it. I knew I shouldn't leave her there!"

"Danny—it probably has nothing to do with this. She had some kind of severe allergic reaction, but the paramedics got there in time— she's at Lancaster General."

"We passed that on the way here, didn't we?"

"Yes, but I'll take you there or you can drive."

But before he could get his keys out of his pocket, Danny was on his feet running.

CHAPTER THIRTY

S am stood for a few moments with his mouth hanging open, shocked to see how fast the boy could run. A dog across the street had tried to chase after the fleeing figure, but Danny left the poor creature behind.

What Sam didn't realize was that all his young life Danny had been outrunning things—the boy had never trained on a track, but the need to get away from bullies, from police officers, from abusive foster parents and occasionally from vendors whose fruit Danny had stolen was an effective way to learn to use his legs—they were Danny's vehicle. Add to that the adrenalin that was currently pumping and Danny was faster than ever. It took him just eight minutes to run the four-and-a-half blocks to the emergency room.

Gasping for breath, he shouted at one of the attendants behind the front desk, "Casey Lewis. Where is she? How is she? What's happened?"

He felt a sharp pain in his side and bent slightly over to ease it. Taking deep breaths, he tried to slow his heart rate and calm his body and his mind. He knew the attendants probably couldn't understand his desperate words. He repeated his queries, trying to keep his voice steady. "I need to find Casey Lewis. Where is she?"

The woman behind the desk, who had looked in alarm at the frantic young man yelling in her direction, snapped into efficiency mode and turned to a computer keyboard. "Is that Louis with an 'OUIS' or an 'EWIS?'" she asked.

"Cassandra L.E.W.I.S." Danny said through gritted teeth.

"Oh, here she is. She's still in the emergency suite, but they're in the process of moving her to a third-floor room. Are you a relative or legal guardian? Only relatives are allowed on the floor."

"I'm her cousin," Danny lied. "Where's the elevator?"

The woman looked Danny up and down, but either believed the lie or decided the handsome young guy was not a threat. She pointed to a bank of elevators, "Take a left when you get off."

Although Danny's legs and mind itched to take the stairs, he decided he needed to maintain the appearance that he was in control of his emotions. He walked calmly to the bank of elevators and pushed a button. The elevator seemed to take forever to reach the floor, and when it did, he finally got on, along with several other people. The elevator seemed to creep up to the second floor where most of the people got out. *Hurry up, hurry up!*

The minute the elevator stopped on the third floor, however, and the door opened, Danny jumped out, turned left and sprinted down the long hall to a desk. "I'm Cassandra Lewis's cousin," he told the nurse. "I need to see her."

"She's being settled now in three B so they can monitor her and continue administering fluids. You can't get in there quite yet. I'll need to see some identification," the nurse said as she looked over at Danny, who looked up at the ceiling in exasperation. He had no driver's license, no credit cards, but then he thought about what he did have in his pockets, looked at the nurse and pulled his old library card from his back pocket.

"I didn't have time to grab my wallet. But here's a picture ID," he said as he held out the card.

"Anything with a name and picture," the nurse said. "Just sign here."

Danny grabbed the pen and scribbled his name. The nurse pushed her chair back from her desk and stood up. "I'll show you to the waiting room, but you can't see her until the doctor and nurse are through."

She led him to the end of a long hall where Joseph sat in one of several brown plastic chairs. Joseph was bowed at the waste, his head almost to his knees, his hands behind his head. As Danny approached, Joseph straightened up, and Danny saw how white the caregiver's face was.

But Joseph stood up and clasped Danny's arm. "She's okay," he assured Danny. "We don't really know what happened. She was eating one of Sarah's muffins, and suddenly she couldn't breathe and starting swelling up. They've got her stabilized, and on oxygen and steroids or something. I haven't been in to see her yet, but I talked to the doctor."

"Who was there, Joseph? Who came to the house?"

Joseph looked confused. He shook his head, and both men sat down.

"No one was there but us, Danny. I don't know what happened, but there were no outsiders at the house. Casey is allergic to only two things that I know of—bees and peanuts. But it's the middle of winter, and we *never* have peanuts anywhere near the house. We just don't allow it."

"We have an epi-pen because of the bees, and I went to the hall desk where she keeps it, but it wasn't there. I don't know where it went," Joseph said. He was wringing his hands. "It's always there." He put both palms over his eyes and rubbed.

Without thinking, Danny put his arm around the older man, who seemed to settle down then. Joseph withdrew his hands from his face and whispered, "Thank God they got there in time."

Danny thought for a minute.

"Where was Sarah, Joseph? Where is she now?"

Again, Joseph looked confused.

"With us the whole time. She took one look at Casey and called the paramedics before I could even react. I rode with Casey in the ambulance. Sarah stayed behind to get the paperwork that gives us medical guardianship for Casey when something happens. I'm sure she's on her way now."

Joseph's face contorted as if in pain. Danny saw tears in the older man's eyes.

"She could have died, Danny. It's like fate has something going for this child. All this attempted murder business, and she ends up in the hospital because of an allergic reaction. I just don't understand it."

He really does love her like a daughter, Danny thought to himself, as he patted Joseph's back.

It was another hour before the doctor came to assure Joseph, Danny, and Sarah that Casey was going to be fine. Sam had visited, but realized the futility of being there. He filled Danny in on what police were doing just to keep the younger man's mind occupied for a few minutes. Neither Anna Mae nor Ricky had been located, but the warrants had been approved for searches of the other executives' houses, which were keeping the police occupied. They'd eventually come to the hospital to interview Casey, but there was no hurry for that.

Danny didn't seem capable of totally focusing on anything but getting into the room to see Casey. Sam noticed, however, that he kept glancing over at Joseph and Sarah as if trying to analyze their reactions and what had happened. The detective left a few minutes before the doctor arrived.

"Casey is going to be just fine. I believe from the severity of her reaction, it must have an anaphylactic reaction to whatever she was eating."

Danny saw Sarah go completely pale and grab Joseph's hand.

"We can analyze the situation later, but save those muffins you gave her Sarah. She must be allergic to something we don't know about. We'll allow a few minutes for you all to visit, but we'd like to keep her overnight. We'll be monitoring her for another few hours, then probably give her a mild sedative to sleep when we know there won't be any further complications. I'd suggest you all say your hellos then go home and get some sleep. Visiting hours ended 10 minutes ago."

Casey's face was still swollen, and she had hives around her mouth, but Danny thought he'd never seen a more beautiful site than the girl propped up in bed, an IV hanging next to her.

Her throat still hurt too much to do anything but whisper.

"Sorrry, Dannny. 'S my fault."

"Casey, for goodness sakes. We don't know what happened, but *you* didn't do anything wrong," Joseph said.

"Oh, honey. I think it was something in those muffins," Sarah said and began to cry. Casey just squeezed her hand.

Danny knew that Casey hadn't been talking about the allergic reaction. She was apologizing for getting upset with him. Without regard to what Joseph or Sarah might think, he simply picked up her hand and kissed the palm. Casey got the message and smiled.

The three of them left Casey 10 minutes later, promising to be there first thing in the morning. The doctor had explained that unless there were complications, she'd be released as soon as possible the next day. Four hours later, Casey was still not able to sleep, and the nurse brought a sedative. Casey sighed deeply as she fell asleep knowing she was cared for not just by Joseph and Sarah anymore, but by the dark-haired, blue eyed, deep-souled man she now knew she loved.

CHAPTER THIRTY-ONE

Casey was buried deep under layers of fog and fighting to come up into the daylight. Her hands reached out but touched only air. Her head pounded, and her skin itched slightly, but she could breathe and for some reason that brought a sense of relief. What had happened? What was that stinging smell?

Her eyes flew open, and she realized she was in a dim room that was not her own. The sheets felt stiff against her skin. Her arm hurt. She looked at the arm and saw a bandage, attached to a tube, running to a plastic bag, hanging by the bed. *I'm in the hospital.*

Casey put her other hand on her aching head, trying to get her mind to focus. She remembered nibbling one of Sarah's delicious bran muffins, taking little bits into her mouth and savoring them. Suddenly, she'd felt—different. Her throat had started closing, her lips felt fat. Her eyes had stung.

Casey rubbed her eyes now and looked around the hospital room. She tried to sit, but got only as far as lifting her head. She remembered Danny holding her hand, then, and she settled back against the pillow and smiled, closing her eyes to return to sleep.

Casey heard a rustling sound and opened her eyes a slit. A nurse had come into the room, and Casey thought about asking her for a glass of water. Her throat felt like it was on fire. But sleep won out over thirst, and Casey began to drift off.

Something didn't feel right. Casey stirred when she felt someone tuck covers around her body and up over her chin, then rest against the bed. She opened her eyes fully.

The nurse was leaning heavily against the bed, almost sitting on Casey shoulders. She was fumbling around in a big bag on her lap. Casey saw her take something long and sharp out of the bag, along with a small bottle. The nurse turned her head, and Casey saw Anna Mae, but the hair and the face were all wrong somehow.

Why is Anna Mae in a costume, and why is she administering medicine?

"Wha—" but Casey didn't quite get the words out.

The bed sheets moved as Casey tried to bring Anna Mae into clearer focus. The older woman felt the movement and turned her head from her task to focus on the girl in the bed.

Casey's vision cleared in an instant, and what she saw shocked her. Anna Mae, who was always so immaculately dressed, wore an ill-fitting uniform, large thick-framed glasses and a light brown, curly wig. But it was the expression that startled. Casey was used to seeing apathy and coldness in Anna Mae's expression, but now Casey was looking into the face of hatred. Anna Mae's eyes were slits; her expression twisted and ugly. The last of Casey's confusion evaporated, replaced by terror. *What is wrong with Anna Mae?*

But before Casey could react, Anna Mae moved the left side of her body further onto the bed, pinning the IV arm under the blanket and shifting most of her weight to Casey's chest. Casey gasped for air and tried to get her other arm out of the blankets.

"Another moment, *dear.*"

Casey tried to squirm from side to side. But Anna Mae had turned her body and was sitting on the struggling girl's chest, neck and head. Casey was trapped beneath covers, her airways covered. She fought as hard as she could to move her shoulders, but Anna Mae's many hours at the gym had paid off. She was stronger than her intended victim.

"I suppose I could just let you smother, but that's not the plan. Then again, you've managed to bungle all my attempts."

Casey managed to free just the top of her head by thrashing it back and forth—her eyes cleared a little, and she looked up through Anna Mae's body, between an arm and the woman's side and saw Anna Mae reach out and inject something into the top of the IV, the needle still in her hand.

Casey's mind couldn't make sense of any of this, but she knew she was in danger. For just a moment, she freed the arm not attached to the needle and brought it up to hit Anna Mae, but the woman just looked around at the source of the strike, and then used her own arm to constrain Casey's.

"Not this time, deary. Not this time. I spent way too much effort and money locating something that will make you finally go away. They'll all say what a tragedy it was that a mere allergic reaction resulted in a heart attack, or maybe you'll just drift away, stop breathing altogether," Anna Mae's cackle was brittle and false, as if she was rehearsing to play the role of the wicked witch.

Casey knew she had only seconds before the liquid reached her veins. She tried to scream, but her scratched throat and Anna Mae's dead weight muffled her attempts. Casey's consciousness was starting to slip from the lack of air, the room becoming black at the edges of her vision.

Suddenly Casey heard a growl, and Anna Mae's weight became unbearable. Instead of being suffocated, Casey knew now that she was about to be crushed by this monster, whose mass suddenly had doubled. But just as suddenly, the weight was gone, though blackness was still dancing around the corner of her eyes. She forced herself to focus, inhaled as much air as she could, and turned her head toward the IV tube that was about to kill her. With extreme effort she swung her free arm over herself to tear at the needle in the other, feeling her own flesh rip just as the darkness won its race. Casey lost consciousness.

"Casey. Casey can you hear me? Casey wake up. It's me, Danny."

This time, when she opened her eyes, Casey saw Danny sitting beside her on the bed. He was stroking her cheek gently. A nurse tapped Danny on the shoulder, but Danny would not budge.

"I need to check her over, Sir. Please let me through."

Casey reached up to touch Danny's face and saw the blood on her arm, on his face, on the sheets. Then she remembered Anna Mae in the nurse's uniform, the look on the woman's face and the strange cackle. She tried again to raise herself, using her other elbow.

"It's okay, honey. You're safe now. We got our killer." Danny looked across the room, and Casey followed his eyes. Anna Mae laid sprawled face first on the floor, her hands bound by handcuffs, a uniformed security guard standing over her. The would-be killer turned over and sat up. Her wig was lopsided now on her head, her makeup smeared, her uniform had streaks of dirt or makeup or blood from her bleeding forehead—Casey couldn't tell. But the look that had terrified Casey earlier remained. The uniformed security guard bent down and helped her to her feet.

Casey looked back at Danny, a question in her eyes. The nurse had managed to shove him aside and was now cleaning up Casey's ripped IV arm. Danny had moved further down the bed to give the nurse access.

"How did you know she was here?"

"I couldn't leave the hospital. They let me stay in the waiting room. I don't know, honey. I don't know how I knew, but I woke from a sound sleep and knew you were in trouble."

"*You little bitch.*" All eyes turned to Anna Mae. The guard held her firmly by the arm, and she didn't even try to struggle, but her breath was coming in gasps as she shouted, "*I cannot believe you did this again.* How the *hell* do you manage to have luck every damn step of the way. You get all Richard the turd-ball's money. You get all Richard the turd-ball's affection. The goddamn bastard leaves me pennies and my own precious boy nothing. And now you think you're gonna just waltz in there and take over the whole *company*? I put twenty-five years into that business. You know nothing about running a drug company," Anna Mae was practically spitting the words out and everyone in the room was too shocked to react.

Her tirade was interrupted, however, by the police. Two officers arrived, and one immediately took Anna Mae's arm from the guard and led her out of the room. The shouting continued as they lead Anna Mae out the door, and her words hung in the air but the volume decreased as the officer led her away.

CHAPTER THIRTY-TWO

A week after Anna Mae was apprehended at the hospital, Sam sat in Casey's living room sharing hot cider with Danny, Casey, Joseph and Sarah. A fire roared in the grate.

Sam spent the week wrapping up what he had found out in his investigation and gathering what the police would tell him so that he could make a final report to Casey.

One thing was different from his last visit to the house: Danny and Casey sat side by side on the sofa loosely holding hands.

The couple had already talked to Sam about Casey's upcoming twenty-first birthday party. Because two of the company's executives were now behind bars, the anniversary gala had been scaled back. But Casey felt it was time she got to know the people that had given so much time to her father's company so she'd decided to hold an employee's-only bash on her birthday.

As Sam sipped the cinnamon-scented beverage, he relaxed back against the overstuffed armchair and thought to himself, *this is the first time we've sat in a room together without the tension of the case between us.* He was pretty sure the rest of the people in that room were feeling the same. Certainly, Casey looked more relaxed than Sam had ever seen her. Her cheeks were pink, her eyes bright. Casey seemed to glow from inside.

Sam smiled as he sipped, glancing from Casey to the young man beside her. But it was time to get down to business. Sam put down his mug and opened his notebook.

"Frankly, I find it hard to believe that Anna Mae forgot that Casey's cell phone was in the pocket of the snowmobile suit she wore the night of the storm. But I'm not sure how clearly she was thinking that night. I'm not even sure she planned the whole bit with the open window. I think she came to the house, then left for home and decided later that night, when she was snowmobiling and maybe had a few drinks, that the storm presented an opportunity.

"Good little cell phone you have there—it was turned off, but the battery stayed alive for almost two weeks!"

Casey's happy glow seemed to fade as she turned from Danny to give Sam's words her full attention.

"Sam," she said. "Something has puzzled me. How could Anna Mae have known I'd be in the hospital when she made that last attempt?"

"I think she put you there. I had those muffins Sarah made analyzed, and the lab found ground up peanuts in the mix. Anna Mae must have mixed peanuts into the wheat bran Sarah uses, probably slipped into the kitchen either right before the snowstorm, during that visit, or right afterward. Sarah says she always made the muffins on Mondays but hadn't gotten around to it since before the storm. Anna Mae must have known that."

"I told you that when the police searched Anna Mae's house, we didn't find anything that connected her directly to the crimes," Sam continued. "But we did find something odd: an emergency vehicle monitoring system. We thought maybe it was a hobby of Ricky's, but we never got the chance to question either of them about it. I guess Anna Mae was waiting for the emergency call."

Casey's eyes dimmed a little further.

"But why, Sam. Why did she want to kill me? She didn't inherit anything directly, though I guess her son would have benefited. It's not like she needed the money. She was making a huge salary at the company."

Sam's soft brown eyes sought her troubled ones. It was time to share what else he'd learned as well as the conclusions he'd drawn.

"Anna Mae was a power-driven woman who learned to use her brain to manipulate people. It made her an excellent sales person for the company, and probably a major contributor to its success. Most of the people I talked to outside the company spoke highly of her. It was only the people from within—those who had to deal with her on a daily basis, that thought she was difficult."

"But what does that have to do with me?" Casey asked.

"Her two main drives were the company and her son. With you out of the way, her son became the majority stakeholder, not to mention the wealth he'd get from Richard's estate."

Casey withdrew her hand from Danny's and rubbed both sides of her forehead.

"So you think Ricky was in on her efforts? Was it a plot between them?"

"No, Casey. I don't think either Ricky or Ginger had anything to do with this. The police investigation will affirm this. They certainly had motive—neither was particularly good at managing the trust funds that came to them, and they were both about to lose their income. Neither has a job, though they have plans to work together on creating comic books. But believe it or not, I think they are happy— together that is."

"I know they're a couple, Sam. They came to see me after Anna Mae was put in jail; and I guess I've suspected for awhile. Ricky has talked about little else but what he and Ginger were doing for a long time."

"God," Casey said softly. "Anna Mae had plenty of income, but she was willing to *kill* me for more wealth and power? I can't imagine her hating me that much or being so driven that she had to completely control the company. She must have known I'd keep her at the helm. The company was doing well."

Sam cleared his throat then and sat back against the chair. He drummed his fingers for a moment against his notebook. Casey noticed his hesitancy.

"What, Sam. What is it?"

"Okay," Sam said as he flipped a couple of pages.

"The day before everything went down at the hospital I found out something that I think was the reason your father changed his will. I'd been tracing his steps leading up to that change. Besides John Hutchins's secretary at the company, I also talked to Wilma Smith, your dad's long-time assistant, who's been retired for five years now from the company—she's one of the ones being honored next week, isn't she?"

"I believe so. What did she tell you?" Casey's eyes were now very round.

"This wouldn't hold up in court without further investigation, Casey, because it's based on one woman's memory and conjecture; but apparently, sometime during the week we know your father went to his lawyer, he received an express package that Wilma signed for. She says she glanced at where it was coming from, and for some reason the name caught her attention. Later, she looked up the company name. Apparently your dad had sent away to one of those companies that does paternity testing. I don't know how he would have gotten Ricky's DNA for a test, but it's not very difficult."

Casey looked like she didn't want to know the rest. Her head was now turned away from Sam. But Sam went on, anyway.

"It's possible he found out Ricky was not really his son. We know Anna Mae had him seven months after she and Richard were married. I know from talking to people that she was pretty wild in those first years at the company. She could have been pregnant when she and Richard started dating, and Richard believed the baby was his. Like I said, we'd need evidence to prove that, but you could probably track it down. I just thought I ought to let you know."

Casey was slowly shaking her head. Danny seemed to sense her sadness and took her hand again. After a few moments, Casey found her voice, "It would do any us any good to find out Ricky is not really my brother. I see no point whatsoever. He's been my brother for all of my life, and I'm keeping it that way," she said.

Sam sat back and sighed. "I will say this: your dad was a pretty honorable man for not disowning Ricky. I guess he also thought it served no purpose. But if Anna Mae knew—it's likely he would have confronted her—it gave her all the more reason to need you gone. She was injecting your IV with a drug called succinylcholine. It's used in small doses to immobilize someone during a medical procedure, but the amount she'd given you would have stopped your body from working—you would have stopped breathing or your heart would have stopped in a short amount of time. It wasn't hard for her to get with her connections, and it's very difficult to trace in an autopsy."

"What about Dad's death? Do you think she had anything to do with that?" Casey asked.

Sam shrugged his shoulders. "She's certainly clever enough, and I have my theories. But we can't prove anything without further investigation, and that would probably start with exhuming your father's body. Lab testing has come a long way in the seven years since he died; it's possible they could find something besides what they included in the initial autopsy report. He was just over the legal limit for drinking so the police wrote it off as an accident. Anna Mae could have slipped something in his drink or somehow tampered with the car in a way that wasn't discovered. Police are questioning her about it, but she hasn't confessed to anything, so unless you want to exhume your dad's body and have it analyzed or the police don't think they have enough to charge her on the current attempts, there's little point in pursuing that case."

"I don't want Dad's body dug up," Casey said. "There's just no point. But what about the expired drugs? Was that connected to all this?"

Again, Sam was quiet for a few moments.

"As you know, John Hutchins has been arrested based on what Anna Mae has told the police. He's apparently been skimming off the top for quite some time, maybe as far back as before your dad died. Anna Mae says she only discovered it recently, but I think she knew and was holding it over his head. I think she also was planning on pinning this whole murder rap on John if it came to that, and that she planted the gun in his house. If we hadn't caught her red-handed trying to get to you, she may have been successful in throwing the attention elsewhere. Meanwhile, the audit will probably uncover what the police need to convict John for embezzling."

Sam leaned forward then, reaching for his mug and taking a swallow. He put the cup carefully back in its saucer before continuing, "So far, however, the police have found nothing that ties John in any way to the expired drugs. And my friend Bob McCoy has told me he was not the person they were investigating."

Casey cocked her head.

"Was in Anna Mae then? Was she also selling drugs on the expired market? I just can't see that at all."

"No, Casey. I'm afraid they are looking at Reggie Stone."

Casey turned very pale then and turned to seek Danny's eyes. Danny withdrew his hand from hers so that he could gently stroke her cheek. Steeling herself, she faced Sam again.

"Uncle Reggie has been selling drugs on the black market." It wasn't really a question. Casey was just trying out the idea.

"I'm giving you a heads up to prepare you, Casey. He hasn't been arrested, but it's coming in the next few days. I probably shouldn't be sharing this information with you. I do know that he's in serious debt from Ellie's many trips to the hospital. I did my own investigation of his finances, and they didn't add up. He's had too many huge chunks of payments to various parties connected with that debt. I had pretty much deducted that he was getting infusions of funds from somewhere.

"I don't think he spent a penny on himself, however, except for that Lexus. But he's been taking care of a sick, bitter woman for many years, and the couple has no other family to help."

"Poor Uncle Reg. I'm afraid he hasn't had much of a life outside of that company. I know that selling expired drugs is very wrong, but I'm sure he didn't intend to hurt anyone. From what you've told me, the drugs that were sold are pain killers and stuff used by college kids as study aids. If he is arrested and prosecuted, I'd like to take on his legal fees."

"Don't get ahead of yourself, Casey, and certainly don't tell this to anyone. I don't think Reggie is a flight risk, but we need to let the police do their job."

"In the meantime, you have a company to take care of. With the first and second in command in jail, I'm afraid they've left behind a mess. What are you plans for your inheritance?"

Casey relaxed then and reached for Danny's hand again.

"My father was proud of the company, but it's time to pass it on to someone who takes the pride in it that Dad did. I plan to get caught up on where everything is, and get to know the employees better; but eventually I want to sell.

"I have no desire to run a company. I certainly have no need for more money. Anna Mae's shares will likely be held up by what's happening with her. But I think I can convince Uncle Reggie to sell his portion of the company.

"I am going to give a big chunk of my fortune away to causes I feel are important. I'll set up trust funds for Ricky and Ginger, but may put in provisions that they must go to school. I know that sounds bossy, but I don't want to see them blow that money again."

"And I intend to set aside a good chunk in case I ever get in the shape Ellie is in,"

A cloud crossed Danny's face. "Casey," he said softly, drawing Casey's attention to his face. His voice gained some volume. "You have no damn reason to believe that you'll ever be like that," he said. "Ellie is very sick. You're perfectly healthy and—"

Casey simply put a finger to Danny's lip to stop his anger.

"This is my decision, Danny. I feel like I've been a burden most of my life and never really done anything."

She turned back to Sam then.

"I don't intend to sit around and do nothing, however. I have decided it's time to finish my business degree and work at least part time somewhere where there are people. It's time I stopped seeing myself as some pitiful character and started seeing how other people live."

"Yeah, it is," Danny said softly, but he smoothed her hair, leaned over, and planted a kiss on her cheek.

Casey continued, "I am really looking forward to working. I'm organized and I love being around people, and I need to be out there doing more things for myself. Joseph and Sarah have agreed to stop hovering over me."

Casey saw a sudden light go on in Sam's eyes.

"I've been looking for a office person with a good head on his or her shoulders so that I can spend some time getting better established here in this community. I need someone personable, presentable, and smart; someone who might enjoy the research aspect of a detective's work. Would you consider working part time for me?"

Casey looked shocked at his words. She tilted her head slightly to let the words sink in. Sam looked surprised at his own words. But he nodded his head as the idea began to crystallize.

"You could finish your degree while you were working. I can't pay a lot, but you don't need a lot."

It was Casey this time who sought Sam's eyes. When she made contact, her face broke out into a huge smile.

"I'm delighted you asked, Sam. It will come in particularly handy because of something Danny wanted to ask you."

Sam looked confused. He turned to Danny, who was also smiling.

"I'm studying online and should have my GED in just a few months. It seems Gus was a pretty good teacher. I've already tested out through the sophomore year."

"That's wonderful," Sam said, and he stood to shake Danny's hand. "And what are your plans now, young man?"

Danny sat just a little straighter, his shoulders erect, his head high.

"I've thought long and hard about what I want to do. I've decided that I want to be on the right side of what's happening in this world. I'm enrolling in the police academy next year, and I'm hoping that you'll help me get in—give me a good recommendation and maybe some advice."

Sam laughed then. "My goodness, I didn't expect to turn you both into crime fighters. But I'd be delighted to help in any way I can."

He moved then to pick up his overcoat, which was draped on the arm of his chair. Both Danny and Casey accompanied him to the front door.

"You'll think about my offer, Casey," he said as he took her hand. To Danny he said simply, "Police academy, huh?" as he put on his coat, then patted Danny on the back.

"Yes. It's really funny when you think about it," Danny said. "Gus spent ten years teaching me how to avoid the police, and now I want to be one of them."

EPILOGUE

Danny sat alone in the vestibule of the small church. He was early, but he hadn't been able to stand another moment in the hotel room. He'd had a fitful, half-awake night of dreams with one vision in particular that kept coming back. In the dream, he'd been in this very church, waiting and waiting for guests to arrive; waiting for Casey and her family. But no one had come. He'd been utterly alone.

Eventually Danny had given up sleep, and got up to shower and make himself a pot of coffee. *This is stupid*, he'd thought to himself. *I'm no longer a little boy, living from meal to meal, shelter to cardboard box.*

I have a plan for my life. I'm going to school. I'm going to the academy. I have a place to live and a woman I love.

What was even more wonderful was that he was certain she loved him back. They'd sat for hours talking of what they could do. Casey was enrolled in college and working for Sam several days a week. He'd received his GED and was starting college-level classes next month, studying criminology in preparation for entering the academy.

Danny had received his driver's license and not only begun driving Casey around, but had encouraged her to drive as well. He'd fit into the Joseph and Sarah and Casey family with ease, forming a square from what used to be a triangle. The four of them cooked together, shopped together, went to the theater.

He couldn't for the life of him figure out why he was so frightened.

Danny stared down the aisle at the florist, who was putting finishes touches on the pew. He watched the camera woman setting up tripods and lighting.

When guests started arriving, Danny left for the chamber where the male half of the wedding party gathered. Twenty minutes later he returned to stand at the front of the church, even more nervous than he'd been before. He stared out at hundreds of faces he didn't know, his nerves zinging and popping.

I guess this best-man business has me spooked.

The music started, and the bridesmaids began their stately walk down the aisle, clutching bouquets and looking as nervous as Danny felt.

The ring bearer brought a moment's relief as the little boy stooped to tie his shoe, setting the pillow with the ring aside and sighing in exasperation. The whole church laughed.

Then Danny saw Casey slowly rolling down the aisle, a vision in soft blue lace, her hair pinned in a gentle bun at the back of her head, adorned with daisies and baby's breath.

He was so proud of her, and together they'd come so far. He'd left his wandering days behind him and used the foundation Gus had begun to build a life. She'd left the remnants of bitterness behind, mended fences with Ginger and Ricky, and learned to face the challenges life had presented. Now here they were best man and maid of honor at Ricky and Ginger's wedding.

Casey saw Danny and her eyes lit with pleasure, and quite suddenly Danny's nervousness disappeared. Casey took her place at the front, the music changed as the guests waited for the bride's arrival, and Danny's eyes made a final sweep of the audience.

At the back of the church, in the very last pew, the only one not occupied by people, Danny spotted an old man. He wasn't dressed for the wedding—had probably wandered in from the street. But despite his ragged appearance, no one seemed to notice. The man was staring not at the entrance in anticipation of Ginger and her father, but straight at Danny.

Despite the distance between Danny and that last pew, Danny felt the heat of the old man's gaze as the man's eyes traveled from Danny to Casey, then back to Danny.

Ask her, boy. She's your fate.

Danny looked over at Casey and put his hand in his pocket to feel the small ring box nestled there. He knew then that all his worries about when she might wake up to realize he was a homeless man, not someone who should be there with her and Jacob and Sarah in the big comfy house were unfounded. The box in his pocket held a tiny diamond, all he could afford for now. But that wouldn't matter to Casey. Danny's face erupted in a joyous smile, and he turned back to face the old man. No one sat in the last pew.

"Thank you old friend," Danny whispered.

ABOUT THE AUTHORS

F. SHARON SWOPE
&
GENILEE SWOPE PARENTE

Aleda Johnson Powell

F. Sharon Swope

F. Sharon Swope began writing when she was ten years old and never stopped. Except for a weekly column in her local newspaper, Sharon never pursued getting her work professionally published. Instead, she married and focused her attention on her four children, all of whom became lovers of reading and writing.

At 82, Sharon realized that if she was ever going to write the books she had in her mind all those years, she had better get started.

Twist of Fate, written in collaboration with her second daughter, Genilee, is her first published book. It is the first of the three-part Sam Osborne detective series. She has also published several short stories in magazines.

Sharon lives with her husband of sixty-four years, Robert, in Woodbridge, Virginia.

GENILEE SWOPE PARENTE

Genilee Swope Parente has made her living writing and editing since she graduated in 1977 with a degree in Journalism from Ohio State University.

Since then, she has worked as a newspaper reporter, in public information offices for a university and a politician, and managed the periodicals for several trade associations. Currently, Genilee works as a freelance consultant writer, allowing her to edit and oversee magazines and newsletters for her clients.

In her free time, she can be found writing a book series for young adults while co-authoring the *Twist of Fate* series with her mother, F. Sharon Swope.

Genilee lives in Dumfries, Virginia with her husband of twenty years, Ray, and her teenage daughter Christina.

FOR MORE INFORMATION ABOUT THE TWIST OF FATE BOOK SERIES OR FOR SPECTACLE PUBLISHING PLEASE GO TO:

www.swopeparente.com

and

www.spectaclepmg.com

or write to:

Spectacle Publishing Media Group
P.O. Box 295
Lisle, NY 13797

To Wanda,

Dreams Do come true!

Genilee Pointe

F. Sharon Swope

CPSIA information can be obtained at www.ICGtesting.com
Printed in the USA
BVOW081539150113

310658BV00002B/11/P

9 781938 444029